"...ow you tell me. Where were you a minute ago?"

"Fantasizing about you in nothing but a pair of glasses" probably wasn't the right answer, so he just shrugged and bit into the now cooler appetizer. The slightly sweet and chewy conch contrasted perfectly with the spice of peppers and crisp batter. "Do you know there are people who have never had a conch fritter?"

She shook her head in mock sadness. "It's a tragedy, really."

"It is. I guess they don't know what they're missing. But still, life can't quite be complete if you don't have good seafood."

A wistful look shadowed her face. "There's a lot to be thankful about in Paradise."

Dylan wanted to punch himself. She'd lived most of her life away from this, and it was obvious she'd missed out on a lot more than seafood while she was gone. He couldn't give her that time back or fix everything that had gone wrong for her, but he could at least try to make her return as welcome as possible. And th_____ ___ ___ _ ____ her, the more determined _

Prop
True lo____

A WEDDING WORTH WAITING FOR

BY
KATIE MEYER

First Published in Great Britain 2016
By Mills & Boon, an imprint of HarperCollins*Publishers*
1 London Bridge Street, London, SE1 9GF

© 2016 Katie Meyer

ISBN: 978-0-263-92028-4

23-1016

Our policy is to use papers that are natural, renewable and recyclable products and made from wood grown in sustainable forests. The logging and manufacturing processes conform to the legal environmental regulations of the country of origin.

Printed and bound in Spain
by CPI, Barcelona

Katie Meyer is a Florida native with a firm belief in happy endings. A former veterinary technician and dog trainer, she now spends her days home-schooling her children, writing and snuggling with her pets. Her guilty pleasures include good chocolate, *Downton Abbey* and cheap champagne. Preferably all at once. She looks to her parents' whirlwind romance and her own happy marriage for her romantic inspiration.

My friends, who try to keep me sane,
and my family who love me even when I'm not.

The Busch Wildlife Sanctuary,
a very special place doing great work.

And Tara, Luke, Stripes and "Tiny Cat"…
my animal inspirations.

And most of all, to coffee.

Chapter One

Usually, the small island town of Paradise lived up to its heavenly name. Today was not one of those days.

Dylan Turner had spent most of the day patching a leaking roof during one of Florida's notorious summer storms, only to have the skies clear the minute he climbed back down onto solid ground. Soaked to the skin and covered in globs of roofing compound that stuck more to his skin than it did to the shingles, he'd done something completely unprecedented in his time as director of the Paradise Wildlife Rehabilitation Center—leave work early.

Now he was headed home smelling like tar, trying to navigate the water-filled ruts in the gravel road ahead of him. Wrenching the wheel hard to the right, he let the four-wheel drive take him up onto the soft shoulder and around a particularly washed-out section. Damn, he might have been better off staying at work after all. In a few hours, the water would have gone down, and there was always more work to do. More than he'd ever imagined when he'd taken the job over a year ago.

Fresh off an MBA from Harvard and ready to return to his home state, he'd thought the job would be a cakewalk, something politically correct to put on his résumé while leaving him plenty of time to surf and hike. Instead he'd found himself working eighty hours a week, often doing things conveniently left off the job description. Things like scooping panther spoor or chopping hundreds of pounds of vegetables. Or roofing repair. Luckily, he'd grown up on a ranch and wasn't afraid of getting his hands dirty.

But the crazy workload wasn't the biggest surprise. No, what had shocked him to the core was how darned much he'd come to love the job—the challenge and the responsibility. He could have worked at a big firm somewhere, but here what he did made a difference. Every dollar he raised, every penny he wrangled for the budget, meant food or shelter for an animal in need, and that was something he could feel good about at the end of the day.

Most days, anyway.

Scratching at a patch of tar behind his ear, he slowed for another puddle, the dirty gray water splashing his windshield and blinding him. He flipped on the wipers and grabbed a swig of the bottled water in the console. Soon he'd be at the turnoff for his cabin, a small two-bedroom right on the edge of the Paradise National Wildlife Refuge. Just a few minutes more and he could have a cold beer and a hot shower.

The ring of his phone cut into his thoughts. Grabbing it out of his pocket, he clicked on the speaker mode and set it on the dash. He needed both hands on the wheel in these driving conditions. Darting a glance at the screen, he saw the name of one of the rehab center's volunteers. Probably calling in sick, although they were supposed to use the office line for that kind of stuff.

"What's up, Jason?"

"I just saw something, something bad, and you were the only person I could think of to call." The teen's voice sounded rushed, as if he was trying to catch his breath.

"Okay." Dylan paused, switching his concentration back to the road as he eased around a fallen branch. "Just tell me what you saw, and I'll see what I can do." Jason was levelheaded to a fault; if he was panicking, there was sure to be a reason.

"Right." There was an audible breath as the kid took a drag on the cigarettes he always had on him. Dylan had been meaning to talk to him about that. "The thing is, it's not hunting season, right?"

"No, not for any of the game animals." The deer and turkey season didn't start until August, and even then there were a lot of rules and regulations as to when, where and how an animal could be taken. Wild boar were always legal, though, and as an introduced species they were a general menace.

"Well, I just saw some guy shoot a deer right out of his truck. I don't think he saw me, I was parked pretty far back under some oaks... Miranda and I wanted some privacy, you know what I mean?"

"Yeah, I know." Teenagers had been making out in the woods for as long as there had been woods. He'd steamed up a few windows himself back in the day.

"Well, anyway, I heard the truck, but didn't think anything of it, figured it was slowing down just because of all the water on the road. But then I heard it—a gunshot."

"You sure it wasn't just a backfire or something?"

"Nah, man. This was a brand-new truck, all tricked out, not the kind you'd expect backfire from. Besides, I saw them load the deer in the bed before they took off."

Hunting out of season was illegal, and so was taking potshots out of your truck like that. "Sounds like poachers. You were right not to interfere. Some of them can be pretty dangerous. But you need to report what you saw to Fish and Wildlife. If you need the number, I can get it for you once I get back to the house."

"Yeah, I know. But here's the thing." Another long drag. "After they left, I saw another deer run into the bushes. Looked just like freaking Bambi, man."

Dylan felt his gut tense. "What do you mean, Bambi?"

"I mean, it was a baby. Dude, I think they shot its mom!"

Dylan bit back a stream of expletives, his jaw so tense his teeth ached. A baby left on its own wouldn't last long. That's why deer season wasn't for another few months, in order to give the fawns enough time to mature. "Are you sure that's what you saw? It wasn't a fox or something?"

"No. It was definitely a baby deer. Can you help it?"

"I'll try." If he could find it. "Listen, where are you, exactly?"

"Right before the turnoff to the wilderness area, on that road behind the canoe rental place."

Dylan knew the spot. It was a natural clearing surrounded by thick old oak trees, and one of the party spots for Paradise Isle's younger crowd. If he took the back road, he could be there in a few minutes. "Listen, Jason, stay put, okay? I'll be right there."

Trying to find a fawn in the scrub and pine forest would normally be like looking for a needle in a haystack. But maybe he'd get lucky. A full day of rain would have left the ground soft enough for tracks, giving him half a chance. He had to at least try. They'd taken in several deer lately, all orphaned by car accidents on the main highway. Tragic, but certainly not purposeful. But this…this was a whole different level of awful.

Passing the turn for his own street, he took the next right, following that around until the gas station Jason had mentioned was in his sights. He parked in the gravel lot behind it, grabbing his daypack from behind the passenger seat before climbing down. He had no intention of staying out long, but he'd had enough backpacking experience to know you never went into the woods without emergency supplies.

Jason was waiting for him, pacing in front of a beat-up car, his girlfriend perched on the hood, eyes glued to her cell phone. "I already called Fish and Wildlife. They're sending an officer out."

Dylan nodded. "Good, they'll want a statement from you. Poaching isn't something they take lightly." He shaded his eyes against the setting sun. There should be another hour of two of daylight, but with the cloud cover it might get dark sooner. Time was running out. "Which way did the fawn go?"

"Um, that way, away from the road."

That made sense. "Can you show me exactly where you saw it?"

"I think so. But, uh, Dylan…"

"What?" Impatient to start, he started in the direction Jason had indicated, forcing the younger man to keep up.

"The Fish and Wildlife people—they said not to do

anything until they got here. Something about preserving evidence, and jurisdiction or whatever."

Dylan rolled his shoulders, hiking his pack up more securely. "If I want to find that deer, I need to look now, before it gets any farther away. So you can tell that officer, if they give you any crap, to hurry and catch up. Hell, they can arrest me if they want, but not until after I find that fawn."

Samantha Finley eased her department-issued F-150 truck to a stop underneath a sprawling oak. She'd been the closest officer when the call came in, but it had still taken her nearly an hour. Budget cuts had left the department spread thin and Sam's assigned area stretched from the coast to the outskirts of Orlando, where she'd been responding to a nuisance alligator report. Only the reptile had turned out to be a partially sunken log, and the reporting homeowner had been so drunk she'd felt tipsy just standing next to him.

Hopefully this wasn't another false alarm. As the newest and youngest officer working in the region, she had a reputation to build, and getting stuck on another wild-goose chase wasn't the way to do it. But then again, better a waste of time than a truly orphaned fawn.

Stepping down from the four-wheel-drive truck, she waved at a T-shirt and jeans-clad teen—Jason Cunningham, according to her notes. He looked nervous, but nodded in response. In her experience, boys his age were never very comfortable around law enforcement, especially if the one packing a gun was a woman.

"Hey, Jason, right?" She extended a hand, and after a second's hesitation he shook it.

"Yeah, that's me."

"I'm Officer Finley. I want to thank you for taking the time to call this in. A lot of people wouldn't have bothered to get involved."

He shrugged his shoulders. "I was just worried about the baby deer."

"I bet. You work over at the wildlife center, right?"

"I volunteer there, yeah. I'm hoping for a scholarship and you have to have a certain number of community service hours. I figure it beats picking up trash."

"I bet. So, can you tell me exactly what you saw?"

She listened carefully, taking down the description of the men and the vehicle. Then she had the girlfriend get out of the car and give her version of events before having Jason walk her to where he'd seen the deer. There were two distinct sets of boot marks, which was consistent with what he'd described. And a long, smooth furrow in the mud where they'd dragged the deer before lifting it up into the truck. Streaks of blood and tufts of tawny fur told the rest of the story. This was the real deal, her first poaching case. She took several photos from different angles, documenting the scene.

"And where was the fawn?"

He pivoted, pointing toward a dense thicket of pines and brush. "It was right there, and then when the truck started it ran back into the woods. I'm really worried about it."

So was she, but she wasn't going tell the kid that. "Hopefully it didn't get far. Either way, thanks for calling it in. I'll contact you if we need anything else from you."

For a minute she thought he was going to say something else, but then he just nodded and loped back to his car. A minute later he was gone, leaving her alone in the clearing. There were two vehicles parked by the gas station, but no one had gone in or come out since she'd arrived, and the only sound was the hum of cicadas in the trees overhead.

It was hard to believe that this patch of wilderness was only a few miles from Paradise's picturesque downtown. But almost half of the island was a dedicated wildlife reserve, a safe haven for an assortment of native wildlife. At least, that was the idea. Today, the reality had been far different. And although logically she couldn't have prevented this, the weight of responsibility was heavy on her shoulders as she made her way to where the boy had last seen the frightened fawn.

Her boots sank in the soft, waterlogged ground, squishing as she pulled them from the mud. Not exactly the best circumstances for a search attempt. There wasn't much daylight left, and the damp dusk buzzed with bloodthirsty mosquitoes. She should have stopped to apply a fresh coat of repellent, but time was running out if she wanted to have any chance of tracking the orphaned deer. So she swatted and swore under her breath as she followed the V-shaped tracks of the fawn.

Weaving her way through between the trees, she kept to the higher and dryer ground on the side of the trail to avoid covering the deer tracks with her own footprints. Twenty minutes in, she'd gone in what her GPS said was nearly a full circle, and was edging up to a gravel access road. There the trail stopped, the ground too rough for tracks.

Would the fawn have crossed it, braving the relative open?

Or stuck closer to the trees and run parallel to the road?

Taking a drink from her water bottle, she made her

way east, checking the soft shoulder for any tracks. Nothing. Retracing her steps, she then went the other way, but there was no sign of the deer. Later tonight, there would be possum and raccoon tracks, but they were just waking up and the dirt was unmarred, washed clean by the earlier rain. Which meant the deer must have crossed the road. Plucky little thing.

Crossing, she scanned the ground on the far side, spotting the tiny tracks heading into a tangle of kudzu vines and trees. "The Vine That Ate the South" was what they called the invasive plant, growing fast and thick across anything that didn't move. A bitch to hike through, but the perfect place for a tired and frightened fawn to hide.

She was halfway to the thicket when she spotted the other tracks. Man tracks. Had the poachers returned?

That didn't make any sense. What would they want with a fawn? Besides, she hadn't seen any other tracks before now. Of course, someone could have kept to the sides of the trail, as she herself had done. The ground was rougher and dryer there, and if she was honest, she hadn't been looking for prints. Her attention had been on the deer tracks.

Resting a hand on her sidearm, a Glock 17, she eased forward more cautiously than before. A second-generation wildlife officer, she'd grown up in these woods and knew how to tread quietly. No need to advertise her presence—not until she knew who she was dealing with.

She ducked under the green canopy of leaves, pushing through the outer layer of vines. Ahead, a narrow game path snaked through the press of branches before opening into a clearing a few yards up. Impressions in the ground marked the progress of both deer and man. For a moment, she wondered if the teen who'd called it in could have come back here while waiting for her, but the prints were too large and deep.

A rustle up ahead stopped her in her tracks. It could be the deer she'd been tracking or some other wildlife. Or it could be a poacher. Drawing her weapon, she moved toward the sound.

Chapter Two

Dylan had actually been starting to feel pretty confident. The tracks were easy to read, and the clouds had broken up, offering some extra daylight. Everything had been better than he'd hoped, right up until he'd slipped on a pile of wet leaves and gone crashing into the underbrush like a drunken tourist. Now he was face down in the muck with mud oozing into places mud should never, ever go. Pushing up, he got his hands and knees under him, then froze.

There, not ten feet away, was the fawn, curled up under the fronds of a cabbage palm, hidden well. Dylan might have walked right by him and never seen him. As it was, he was nearly eye level with the little guy. Or girl; too hard to tell from here.

Easing up slowly, he slid one foot toward it, then another. The deer blinked at him, but didn't move. Most fawns were pretty easy to handle away from their mamas. And this one was too tuckered out to be much of a problem. At least, Dylan hoped so. Holding his breath the last few feet, he eased down into a squat in front of the bedraggled creature. A curious sniff, and then a startled sneeze. "Yeah, I know, I don't smell very good. But I'm here to help, I promise."

As if accepting his words or more likely, too tired to protest, the orphan simply sighed.

"Good boy. Now I'm going to get us out of here, okay?" In a move he'd learned on his parents' ranch, he lifted the deer up onto his shoulders. "There we go. Let's go get some chow. I don't know about you, but I'm starving."

"Freeze." The voice came from directly behind him, feminine but commanding.

Damn it.

He froze, half crouching, half standing. "I can explain…"

"First, put the deer down."

"I don't think that's a good idea, ma'am."

"It's Officer, not ma'am."

"Excuse me, *Officer*," he corrected, his muscles straining at the awkward position he'd been forced to hold. "But I'm guessing you're here for this fawn, same as I am. And if I set him down he's liable to take off again." Probably not, given how tired the little guy seemed, but it could happen. "So if you don't mind, I'd rather just hold on to him and save all of us the trouble."

"Why don't you tell me what you're doing out here, and then I'll decide what happens next."

"Can I at least stand up, so we can talk face-to-face?"

"Slowly. No sudden moves."

Taking her at her word, he straightened, his hamstrings protesting at the slow pace. Nothing like a sustained squat before deadlifting a deer to round out the workday. Once upright he turned to find one of the most attractive women he'd ever seen holding a gun on him.

"Think you could put that away?"

She kept the gun steady. "You said you had an explanation."

Fine. "I'm the director of the Paradise Wildlife Rehabilitation Center. One of my volunteers saw some poachers kill this guy's mama, and called me to see if I could help."

Her dark, almond-shaped eyes relaxed a bit. "Do you have any ID on you?"

"In my back pocket."

She nodded, her ponytail of coffee-colored hair bouncing at the movement. "Get it."

He complied, grabbing his wallet and holding it out so she could see his license as well as his work ID. "I'm licensed with the state. I've got a copy of my permit back in the truck if you need to see it."

She lowered the gun, holstering it before answering. "I'll need to see it before letting you leave with the deer, and I'll need your statement."

"Yes, ma'am. I mean, *Officer*." The fawn squirmed and he tightened his grip. "I just want to get this guy back to the center and then go home, that's all."

She nodded curtly, then turned on her heel and headed back out the way they'd come. "If someone had told me you were going to be out here, we could have avoided… any complications."

"Sorry, I thought Jason would have told you. I know you guys usually want to be first on the scene, but—"

"But you figured the rules don't apply to you?"

"No, but I thought finding the fawn was more important. I had no idea how long it would take for someone from Fish and Wildlife to get here, and didn't want to lose the daylight. Playing by the rules could have meant losing the fawn."

She stopped, her shoulders straightening. "I do get that. Saving the fawn was a priority, for both of us. But next time, let the authorities know if you're going to be tramping around a crime scene."

"Trust me, I don't plan on making a habit of it." He shifted the deer, his tight back muscles reminding him that he'd spent the day nailing shingles. "Believe it or not, this wasn't how I planned to spend my evening."

She looked him over, no doubt taking in the wet and filthy clothes and tar-crusted hair, and for the first time a real smile played on her lips. "What could possibly have been better than this?"

He smiled back. "A beer and a hot shower, in that order." His stomach grumbled. "And food. Maybe a pizza, maybe some television. Not deer wrangling, and definitely not having a gun pulled on me."

Sam felt her cheeks heat. That hadn't gone the way she'd planned. "Like I said, the rules are there for a reason. Going off on your own, half-cocked, when there are poachers around—"

He held up a hand and grinned, his white teeth in stark contrast to his tanned skin. "Hey, no hard feelings. You did what you had to do."

"Exactly."

"And so did I. And hey, it all turned out all right in the end."

She started to argue, but there was no point in antagonizing him. At least he wasn't going to give her grief about drawing her weapon. Yes, she'd followed protocol, but a civilian complaint would still look bad on her record. Not to mention the paperwork it would mean. She had enough of that as it was.

Besides, she needed to maintain a good rapport with the locals. She'd been born here on Paradise Isle, but between boarding school and college she'd spent too many years on the mainland to be considered an islander anymore. Time and distance had made her an outsider, and since she relied on tips like the one the volunteer had called in today, gaining the trust of the residents was her top priority. And given that she'd just threatened to shoot one of them, she had her work cut out for her. Time to take it down a notch and try to defuse the situation.

Of course, it would be a bit easier to relax and make nice if he was more normal-looking. Maybe even a bit homely. But no, he had to be drop-dead gorgeous: tall, with broad, athletic shoulders and a lean swimmer's build. She pegged him for a surfer. He had the sun-bleached shaggy hair and perfect tan that seemed typical of the beach bum crowd, with ocean-blue eyes that crinkled when he smiled. He definitely didn't look like the director of a nonprofit, and truth be told, his movie-star looks were a bit intimidating.

They came out of the woods behind the gas station just as the sun slipped beneath the horizon. Dylan moved past her in the dim twilight, heading for an old, beat-up pickup parked beside the gas station. There were what looked like dog kennels in the back, the kind used for airline travel, lashed in place with cables. Without a word he lifted the baby deer from his shoulders and tucked it into the largest cage, securing the latch with a sigh. "I'll take him back to the center, get him fed and settled in for the night."

She tried to smile around what felt like a dismissal. "I still have some questions for you. For my report."

He shrugged and raised the tailgate. "Well, then, I guess you're coming, too—Officer." He gave a mock salute before climbing in the cab of his truck and driving off.

Sam counted to ten twice as she made her way back to her patrol vehicle. What an arrogant...well, arrogant pretty much summed it up. The man oozed confidence from his pores. She was in full uniform, carried a badge and had even drawn her weapon, but he'd been the one in control of the situation, from start to finish. Even covered in mud, he had a bearing that demanded respect. Meanwhile, she still felt like she was playing dress-up half the time. Maybe her instructor at the academy had been right; maybe she wasn't cut out for this line of work. But damn it, she'd aced her course work and held her own in the physical tests, as well. She'd even broken the academy record for sharpshooting.

She'd worked hard to prove her instructor wrong, to prove that she had what it took. So why did she still let guys like this get to her? He hadn't even done anything particularly awful. Yes, he should have waited for law enforcement to get there, but even she could see his motives were good. And he'd stayed calm and relaxed even when she'd been sweating bullets. Maybe because he had the kind of easygoing confidence she'd always envied. The kind that came from really knowing yourself and being comfortable in your own skin. That was something she hoped to find for herself, and one of the reasons she'd come back to the only true home she'd ever had.

Getting in her car, she checked the GPS. The rehab center wasn't far, and if she hurried she could pick up some food first. An "I'm sorry I almost shot you" gesture. On the other hand, she didn't want him to think this was something other than professional. Friendly was good, flirting was not.

Shaking her head at her own indecision, she started the engine and rolled down the windows. Maybe some fresh air would clear her head. She'd initially been drawn to law enforcement because of her father's involvement, but the clear lines between law and order, right and wrong resonated with her. Unlike some of her fellow officers who chafed at following protocol, she found freedom in following the rules. Rules created order out of chaos. Rules made her feel in control. Without rules, anything could happen, which was probably why she'd reacted so badly to him tracking all over her crime scene. That, and her inner teenager's reaction to a hot guy. Neither was an excuse she felt like sharing.

Letting her stomach do the thinking, she pulled into Lou's Pizza. She needed to eat dinner at some point anyway—might as well share.

Inside, the tangy aromas of tomato sauce and pepperoni tickled her nose, bringing back memories of Saturday night pizzas with her dad. Once upon a time, they'd made it a weekly tradition, just the two of them. That was before her mother died, before the close relationship she'd had with the man she'd worshipped as a hero had degraded into long-distance phone calls and painfully awkward visits home.

Now that she was back in Paradise, she was going to

change that. After all, if she couldn't win over her own father, what chance did she have with the townspeople?

Dylan's hands were kept busy over the next half hour as he dealt with the logistics of caring for an orphan fawn, but his mind was focused on the sexy wildlife officer who'd almost shot him. Shoveling clean shavings into a pen, he wondered what was wrong with him. She'd been armed, rude and way too uptight to be his type. He liked free spirits, women who knew how to let loose and have fun. Women who understood that life was about finding happiness while you could.

He wasn't sure Officer Finley—he'd seen her name on the badge—even knew what fun was. All work, no play was the vibe she gave, with her perfectly pressed uniform and no-nonsense ponytail. No jewelry, no noticeable makeup. Of course, she hadn't needed any, not with her looks. She almost had an exotic appeal, like a buttoned-up version of Angelina Jolie. He had a way with animals and women, and something told him there was a vixen hiding behind that badge.

The fawn pushed up against him, demanding attention.

"All right, I get it. You're almost as bossy as she was." He took a minute to smooth down the bedding, and then headed toward the main building, the animal tottering along beside him. He was just about to unlock the door when the sound of gravel crunching announced a visitor. He'd wondered if she'd show. He waved, then waited as she climbed down, then opened the back door and pulled out a flat white box. Oh, holy hell. She'd brought food.

"If some of that's for me, you can arrest me right now and I won't resist."

She startled for a second, then shrugged and grinned. "You said you wanted pizza, and I hadn't eaten yet, so..."

"So you took pity on me. I wouldn't have thought I liked pity, but if it comes with pepperoni I think my ego can handle it."

"Pepperoni and sausage."

"My angel of mercy. Come on in." He held the door for her, flipping on the lights to illuminate the way-too-small office area that served as command central. He pointed to the largest of the cheap metal desks. "You can sit at my desk if you like. I've got to go finish up with the fawn, but it shouldn't take me very long."

"I can help, if you like. Might go faster with two people."

That he hadn't expected. Maybe he was right, and she wasn't as standoffish as she pretended to be. "Sure, another set of hands is always welcome here."

Picking up the fawn, who had curled up on the floor at his feet, he headed for the door at the rear of the room. "The treatment area is back here."

Without being asked, she flipped the switch by the doorway, flooding the large utilitarian space with fluorescent light. Twice the size of the office and reception area, the room boasted stainless-steel counters, refrigerators, an industrial washer and dryer, and several examination tables. One full wall was taken up by cages of various sizes, only one of which was occupied. The current resident, a tortoise with a wounded foot, looked up and then promptly went back to sleep.

Dylan put the fawn down on a large walk-on scale and made a mental note of its weight. He'd fill out a treatment form for him once he was settled. "Officer, could you keep an eye on our furry friend here, while I mix up some formula for him?"

"Sure." She took his place at the orphan's side, stroking the dappled fur.

He moved to the back counter, where the milk replacement powder and bottles were kept. "You know, if we're going to eat pizza together, maybe you could tell me your first name? It seems a bit formal to keep calling you Officer."

She bit her lip, obviously more comfortable with that layer of formality between them, before nodding reluctantly. "It's Sam, Sam Finley. I guess I didn't get around to introducing myself before."

"No worries." He knew when to back off, when to stop pushing. She was as skittish as the fawn, more so really. The little deer had already started bonding with him. She, however, was doing that one-step-forward, two-steps-back thing that he often saw in the animals they took in. Better to let things lie for a bit, rather than scare her off.

He mixed up the powder with warm water, then screwed the top on the bottle. "Want to try feeding him?"

She looked up, eyes wide. "Me?"

"Sure. It's not hard, and he might appreciate a woman's touch. He certainly seems taken with you."

She looked down to where the fawn was practically wrapped around her legs, then reached for the bottle. "Just tell me what to do. I don't want to hurt him."

He handed it to her. "You won't. Just tickle his lips with it a bit, and hold on tight."

She started to crouch down to the fawn's level.

"No, up high. Remember, the mama deer would be standing up." He guided her arm up into the right position, surprised by the firmness of her biceps and by the heat that shot through him at the casual touch. She was stronger than he'd realized, and more potent, too. Like aged whiskey, she packed a quiet punch.

Leaning against the counter, he watched as she coaxed the deer. Her smile was back, and when the hungry baby head butted her clumsily she actually laughed out loud. "Careful, or I'm going to start think you're a nice person."

She looked up, startled. "Excuse me?"

"First you bring pizza, now you're helping out and enjoying it. Laughing even. What happened to the by-the-book wildlife officer that held me at gunpoint?"

Chapter Three

Sam turned back to the deer, her shoulders stiffening. "You're right. I'm on duty, I should let you do this so I can do what I need to do. Then I can get out of your way."

"Hey, I'm just teasing." He motioned for her to stay where she was. "I mean, you do seem different, but in a good way. No offense, but you were giving off a very different vibe out there in the woods."

"Maybe because it was a crime scene?"

He shook his head, rejecting her defense. "No, I mean, sure, that explains some of it. But you're doing it again right now, putting up some kind of virtual keep-out sign. Which, hey, if that's the way you want it, is fine. We can go back to the cops-and-robbers routine if you like that better."

No, damn it, she didn't like that better. Keeping people at a distance was exactly the opposite of what she was supposed to be doing. Old habits died hard, but if she was going to learn to connect to the citizens here, to earn the kind of trust she needed for her job, she needed to find a way to be more approachable. Too bad she had no idea where to start.

Realizing he might be mistaking her silence for agreement, she said the first thing that popped into her head. "I'm kind of out of practice when it comes to making friends." Pathetic, but true.

But he didn't laugh, or question her statement. Just shrugged. "I'm out of practice when it comes to following orders, if that helps. Not a lot of perfect people walking around. But I think you might be better at making friends than you think." He pointed at the fawn, who had finished the bottle and was now curled up on the floor, his head on her foot, fast asleep.

"It's easier with animals. They don't expect you to know about the latest fashions or which pop singer is divorcing which reality star."

He laughed, and her breath caught in her chest. Energy and beauty radiated from him like warmth from the sun. He was everything she wasn't. And he didn't even know it.

"I think maybe you've been hanging out with the wrong crowds of people, if you think that's what they want to talk about."

"I haven't been doing a lot of hanging out at all. Work keeps me pretty busy."

"Uh-huh." He moved in closer, then bent and scooped up the sleepy fawn. "Most people, at least the ones worth knowing, are looking for the same things the rest of the living world wants. Someone to stick by them, someone they can trust and, yeah, someone to have fun with."

"It's that last part that I need to work on." Why was she telling him all this? He obviously had no idea what it was like to be on the outside looking in.

"Maybe you just need a bit of practice. Having fun, I mean." He moved toward another door, across the room from where they'd come in, somehow managing the knob and the deer at the same time. She followed him out onto a mulched path leading to a set of enclosures. He stopped at one of the smaller ones, empty except for a thick layer of woodchips and a bucket of water. "Your room, sir." The spindly-legged fawn sniffed around the small fenced area, then curled back up and closed his eyes.

"No insomnia for him," Sam commented, with no small amount of envy.

"Nope. He's got a belly full of food and a safe place to sleep. He'll be fine."

"Thanks to you." She looked up at Dylan, daring to make eye contact in the dim starlight. "I'm glad you didn't listen to me, that you went after him. Sorry I gave you such a hard time."

"No worries. You can make it up to me by catching the lowlifes that shot his mother."

Her shoulders dropped. "I'll try. Trust me, there is nothing I'd like more than to put handcuffs on them. But your friend didn't get the license number, and there are a million tan Ford pickup trucks in this part of the state. My best chance at catching them is for someone to turn them in."

"Does that happen often?" He locked the gate on the pen, then headed back to the main building, motioning her to follow.

"Actually, it does. There are some pretty big rewards for tips that lead to an arrest. One of the secrets to being a good wildlife officer is having a personal connection with the community. If you have enough people that know you and trust you, then they can be an excellent source of information. That's why I was assigned here, in Paradise. I was born here, so the brass assumed I'd have a natural connection with the townspeople."

He led them back to the office area and flopped down in a chair. "That makes sense."

Sitting across from him, she opened the pizza box and grabbed a slice. "On paper, yes. In real life, not really." She took a bite and let the flavors roll across her tongue. If heaven was a food, it would be pizza. Chewing, she debated how much to share. "I actually only lived here until I was ten. After that I went to boarding school, and then college. Other than a few school vacations, I haven't been in Paradise in over a decade."

"Have you been able to connect with any old friends from back when you lived here?"

She shook her head. "When you're a kid, it's out of sight, out of mind—I lost touch with everyone years ago. So now I'm starting from scratch, unless you count the town librarian. I spent a lot of time hiding out there the few times I did make it home."

Dylan swallowed the last of his slice. "Bookworm, huh? Remind me to show you my bookshelves sometime." He waggled his eyebrows in a parody of seduction. "But I can see how that would make things awkward. Making friends in a new place is hard enough. Making friends in a place where everyone already knows you, that's a whole different thing."

"Exactly. I'm the new girl in town, except I'm not."

"What about your family? Are they still local?"

The bite of pizza in her mouth was suddenly hard to

swallow. Folding her hands in her lap, she forced herself to answer the question; her family history wasn't exactly a secret in Paradise. "My mom died when I was a kid."

"I'm sorry." The words were ones she'd heard many times, but she could tell he was sincere.

"Yeah, well, after that Dad just kind of shut down—hence the boarding school. He's actually with the FWC as well, but when she passed he took a desk job. He spends pretty much every waking hour holed up in his office in Ocala. Not much time for friendships." Or his daughter. "I know that sounds like the pot calling the kettle black, but at least I'm trying to put myself out there."

"You'll figure it out." He helped himself to another slice.

"I'm going to have to. I can't do my job properly otherwise." Something her boss had made very clear to her during a private meeting last week. "I've got an evaluation coming up, and basically, if I don't create some ties to the community, I'm going to be looking for another line of work."

Dylan coughed, nearly choking on the bite of sausage in his mouth. "What? They can fire you for not being social enough?" She seemed competent, had tracked him and the deer like a pro and was a natural with animals. So what if she was a bit awkward with the two-legged variety?

"Pretty much. There's a big push in the Fish and Wildlife Commission to be what they call community partners. And my boss is spearheading the effort. If I can't make myself a part of that, then I'll be reassigned to an administrative role."

"I'm guessing that's not a step up, careerwise."

She shook her head, her nose wrinkling. "Definitely not. It would be a sign of failure."

She certainly didn't seem like someone accustomed to failure. "So what, you just have to make some friends, get to know the locals, that kind of thing?"

"Pretty much. The Outdoor Days Festival is coming up, and my boss will be here for the opening ceremonies. My plan is to be able to mingle well enough by then to impress him."

"Okay, that sounds like a good plan."

"Yup. And if I had any idea how to make it happen, I'd be doing okay. As it is, I think this is the second-longest conversation I've had since I moved back here months ago."

"I'm flattered. But I've got to know, who beat me out?"

"My cat."

"Ouch."

"Yeah, well, like I said, it's easier with animals. But this is definitely my longest human-to-human interaction."

"Well, that's something, anyway." He grabbed two bottles of water from the case stashed next to his desk and tossed her one. "But technically, this is work-related. What you need is a social life."

She grimaced and took a swig of water. "I've heard of those."

He shook his head. She had a dry wit he hadn't expected—what other surprises was she hiding? "It's not so bad, you know. Some people even find socializing fun."

"Fun is hiking in a forest at dawn or figuring out who did it in the middle of a mystery novel."

"Sure. But fun is also seeing a movie and then talking

about it with friends over ice-cream sundaes. Or picnics on the beach, or a pickup game of volleyball."

She shrugged. "It's not that I don't like people, but a full college course load, plus a part-time job, didn't leave much time for a social life. Now that I've got the time, I don't have the connections. I can't exactly walk up to someone I don't know and ask them to go see a movie."

"Maybe not, but you could go with me."

Her jaw dropped open. "Wait, what?"

"I said, you could go with me. I could even bring a few friends, make it a group thing."

"But why would you do that?"

Because you're smart, sexy and I like hearing you laugh. "Why shouldn't I? I mean, besides the fact that you nearly shot me."

Sam chewed her bottom lip; the simple move sent his blood southward. Not good—just making friends was hard enough. If she realized he was attracted to her, she'd probably bolt. Giving her time to think, he grabbed the new animal intake forms and set them on the desk next to the pizza box. He could fill one out for the fawn while she asked him whatever questions she had. By the time he sat back down, she had a determined set to her shoulders and a gleam in her eye.

"Okay. I'll do it. But nothing too crazy, okay?"

"Fair enough, we'll ease you into things." He looked down at the nearly empty box between them. "How about pizza? I'll bring a few friends, totally low-key." He'd rather it be just the two of them, but that would defeat the whole point. "I'll handle everything. You just need to show up."

She shook her head, but there was a smile on her lips. "Never let it be said I turned down a chance for pizza.

Just let me know when and I'll be there. In the meantime, I really do need to ask you a few questions about tonight."

And just like that she was all business again, her smile giving way to lines of concentration.

"You said Jason called you a little before five. Were you here at the center when you got the call?"

"No, I left work early today, so I was driving home by then."

She raised an eyebrow at that. No doubt Ms. All-Work-and-No-Play never left early. "I had been working on the roof all day, in the rain. I was filthy and soaking wet. I thought I'd run home and shower, and then do some work on my laptop later." He was being defensive, but darn it, he didn't want her to think he was a slacker. He got that enough from people. Usually it didn't bother him, but with her it rankled.

"Okay, so when you spoke with him, what did he say?"

Dylan repeated what he remembered of the short conversation.

"And what was your advice to Jason?"

"I told him to stay put and call the Fish and Wildlife hotline."

"Thank you for that. Not everyone would have known whom to contact. For that matter, a lot of people wouldn't have wanted to get involved at all."

Dylan deflected the praise. "Jason's a good kid. He wanted to do the right thing."

"I could tell. Of course, that doesn't explain why you drove over there yourself, rather than just letting the authorities handle it."

He shrugged. "He asked me to come and try to find the deer. He was worried about it. I was, too, once he told me. Given how thin the FWC is spread, I wasn't sure how long he'd have to wait for an officer to get there. And if I hadn't come, he might have tried to go after it himself. I didn't want him wandering around in the woods at dusk—not with poachers in the area."

She rolled her eyes. "And yet you had no problem doing exactly that yourself."

"I'm not some teenager. And it all turned out good in the end. The deer is safe, Jason's safe and I got to have dinner with a beautiful woman."

Sam adjusted the rearview mirror in her truck and took a hard look at herself. Staring back at her was the same pale skin, brown eyes and oversize mouth she'd always seen. Beautiful? He probably just meant it in some casual, meaningless way. The kind of compliment he gave to everyone.

But it was a first for her.

She stuck her tongue out at herself and moved the mirror back in position before starting the car. No one, other than her father, had ever called her beautiful. She'd spent her teen years hidden behind thick glasses that only amplified the bushy eyebrows she'd inherited. Before college she'd switched to contacts and set up a standing appointment for an eyebrow wax. But she never quite managed the art of makeup, or fashion, for that matter. The few dates she'd gone on had been with boys as nerdy and driven scholastically as she was.

In comparison to them, Dylan was in a whole different league. One she couldn't hope to play in.

Except he'd specifically invited her to see him again, socially. Which was terrifying. Not because he was scary in and of himself—after her initial bout of nerves had worn off, he'd been surprisingly easy to be around. Maybe that was why the animals liked him so much. But he'd be bringing other people, strangers, and this time she wouldn't have work to talk about. She'd have to make actual conversation. Small talk. With people she didn't know.

Why had she agreed to this?

Oh, yeah, because she didn't have a choice. She certainly hadn't made any inroads on her own. Having someone like Dylan along to smooth the way was her best chance. It was pretty ironic, really. She was the one who had grown up here. She should be the one helping him get to know people, not the other way around. But maybe it was best this way. Having him along would mean she could ease past that "Don't I know you?" stage that she kept getting stuck in. It seemed she was always on the edges of people's memories, enough to look familiar but not enough for them to actually remember who she was. And once they were reminded that she was actually an island native they invariably felt bad for not remembering her. Not exactly the best way to start a new friendship.

But Dylan's plan was going to work. It had to. She couldn't risk losing her job over it. She'd be humiliated, and her father would be so disappointed. How many times had he told her that she'd have to work extra hard to prove herself? Aside from fighting any suggestions of nepotism, she was a woman in what had traditionally been a man's job. The old-boy network hadn't died out yet and he'd warned her she'd have to prove herself every step of the way. And she had. No way was she going to let a little shyness keep her from doing what she'd always wanted to do. The woods and waterways of Florida were home to her, and she'd sworn to protect them. She just hadn't realized that the hardest part of the job wouldn't be the long hours, dangerous animals or ravenous insects. Somehow, in her rush to be the best, she'd missed the memo about the importance of community relations. At least she had someone on her side now.

And as crazy as it was, she was kind of looking forward to having dinner with him. Not that she expected anything from him other than moral support and some social introductions. But it would be nice if they could form a kind of friendship, as unlikely as that seemed, given how different their personalities were. But they both were dedicated to the wildlife of the area—maybe that would be enough?

More intimidating was the thought of the friends he was bringing. If this was any other kind of challenge, she'd know how to prepare, but she couldn't exactly study up on small talk. Could she? There probably wasn't an official guidebook, but the internet was a big place, and there might be something there that would help. Heck, if she could learn how to change her own oil from a You-Tube video, anything was possible.

The driveway of her apartment building came into view, and she parked in front of her tiny unit. Grabbing her gear, she purposely avoided looking at the wilting plant in front of her door. An impulse buy, it was now a testament to her lack of a green thumb. Half the time she forgot to feed herself; a plant didn't stand a chance. Her cat, on the other hand, was in no danger of neglect, thanks to his in-your-face style of negotiation. She could hear him now, meowing impatiently as she unlocked and opened the door.

The angry meows became rumbling purrs as the fat orange feline wound his round body through her legs, greeting her the same way he did every evening. Careful not to trip over him, she made her way to the kitchen to boot up her laptop and feed her hungry pet. "Don't worry, Cheesy, I'm getting it. It's not like you couldn't stand to miss a meal."

He meowed in protest, no doubt offended at the suggestion he could stand to lose a pound or ten. She really should put him on a diet. But not tonight. She'd add feline obesity to her list of things to look up online. For now she gave him fresh water and a small can of wet food, his nightly treat.

Cat duties finished, she slid onto a stool at the breakfast bar and pulled up a web browser. Her fingers hovered over the keyboard—was she really going to do this?

Yes.

Refusing to hesitate anymore, she typed "how to make a good first impression" into the search box and hit Enter.

Chapter Four

Dylan checked the dashboard clock as he pulled his truck into one of the few vacant spots in front of Pete's Crab Shack. He was early and would have been earlier if he hadn't changed shirts three times before leaving the house. Since moving to Paradise, he'd happily let his wardrobe drift from business button-downs to beach casual, the laid-back dress code being one of the better perks of his job. But tonight his ingrained preference for comfort had been overridden by his desire to make a good impression, costing him both time and a good chunk of his masculine pride. The idea of getting "dressed up" had always seemed fussy to his ranch-raised way of thinking, but having dinner with Sam was enough of an occasion that he'd dug out a collared shirt from the back of his closet. He'd even ironed it, much to the amusement of the neighbor he'd had to borrow the iron from.

Even still, he seemed to have arrived before Sam and Dani. Hopefully, the two women would hit it off—he wanted Sam to feel comfortable in Paradise for reasons he wasn't going to begin to contemplate. Dani Post, like Sam, was a Paradise native, but there the similarities ended. Unlike Sam, Dani was outgoing and bold, characteristics that served her well in the courtroom. As a public defender, she had a soft spot for anyone she considered the underdog, and was on the board of pretty much every charity in town. And with her contacts she was the perfect person to help Sam. He'd first met her at a fund-raiser for a new fox enclosure at the rehab center, and they'd quickly become friends. Once or twice, he'd considered asking her out, but they didn't have that kind of chemistry and they both knew it.

A chime at his hip alerted him to an incoming call. Climbing out of the truck, he headed for the entrance as he answered. "Hello?"

"Hey, Dylan. It's Dani. I'm afraid I've got to back out of dinner. Mollie and Noah have dinner reservations to celebrate her newest gallery show and their babysitter called in sick."

Dani's sister, Mollie, was a longtime volunteer at the rehab center and a gifted wildlife photographer. She'd recently married a sculptor from Atlanta and adopted his young son. Together they had a great little family, but for a pair of newlyweds they didn't get much alone time. "No problem. I know when I'm outclassed. I can't compete with your nephew."

"Well, he is a lot cuter than you. But I still feel bad for ditching you."

"You should. Now I'm going to have to dine all by

my lonesome with a beautiful woman. How will I ever survive such a fate?"

Dani chuckled at his sarcasm. "Good point. My conscience is clear. But do give her my number, and tell her that I'm happy to help however I can."

He'd made it to the front entrance and could see Sam's truck pulling into the parking lot a few rows back. "I will, don't worry. You're not totally off the hook. But she's here now, so let me go."

Hanging up, he watched Sam hop down from her shiny pickup with the grace of a queen stepping down from her throne. She was wearing a long cotton skirt that clung to her legs as she walked and a slim, sleeveless shirt that was at once both modest and seductive. Of course, she'd been sexy in her bulky uniform, too, but this took it to a whole other level. Even her hair was different, loose and flowing in soft waves past her shoulders instead of in the no-nonsense ponytail he remembered. Sam in professional mode was hot. Sam in a skirt was heaven come to earth.

She spotted him and waved, her long legs skimming over the asphalt with the same athletic stride he'd seen in the field. He waved back, and sent up a prayer of thanks for sick babysitters.

She stopped a few feet away, rocking back on her heels to look up and meet his gaze. "So, where's our third?"

"Actually, it looks like it's just going to be us."

Sam arched one perfect eyebrow, her arms crossed over her chest. "I thought the point of tonight was to introduce me to some of the community."

"It was. And it is, I swear. But my friend—Dani—had to cancel. She just called, or I would have let you know sooner. She has to watch her nephew tonight."

"Uh-huh." What he'd come to think of as her work face locked in place, her gaze focused on his as she searched for any deception.

"You can call her if you don't believe me. In fact, she made me promise to give you her number. She really does want to help. But family comes first, it seems."

Sam's expression softened. "I can't argue with that."

"Good. Then you'll still have dinner with me?"

She shrugged. "I'm hungry, so sure. Why not?" She started up the wooden stairway that led to the restaurant's main deck. "But no more surprises, okay?"

He let out the breath he'd been holding and started up after her. He'd promise pretty much anything if it would get keep her from leaving. "No surprises. Scout's honor."

Sam didn't doubt that the capable outdoorsman had been a Boy Scout, but she had a feeling the surprises weren't over yet. She certainly hadn't expected that little flutter of anticipation in her belly when she'd found out they'd be dining alone together. Or the outright relief that had flowed through her when she realized he wasn't going to cancel just because his friend couldn't come.

Pretty much every feeling she had around him was a surprise, and it wasn't likely that was going to change, no matter what he promised. Oddly, that was almost part of the excitement. Somehow he had a way of getting her out of her comfort zone, and she'd certainly worn quite a rut for herself there.

Dylan reached her side and gestured across the expanse of covered deck toward the smaller, enclosed dining room. "Inside or out?"

"Out, definitely." From what she remembered, only a few elderly diners or tourists ever ate inside. Even on a hot day, fans and a sea breeze kept the patio from being stifling, and the view more than made up for the temperature. Beyond the patio railing, the ocean stretched as far as the eye could see, green in the shallows, then darker blue, with tufts of white foam where the waves collapsed on a hidden sandbar. Above, pelicans circled and dove, fishing for their dinner a few feet away from the wooden trestle tables where the diners enjoyed theirs. This place was exactly what she thought of when she'd lain awake homesick in boarding school. Sea, sky, food and people who cared more for who you really were rather than what brand of jeans you wore or car you drove. Here, there was no pretense. Here, everyone fit in. Everyone but her.

"Is this okay?" Dylan nodded to a table nestled in a corner of the deck, open to the water on two sides.

"Perfect." And it was. Far enough away from the center of activity to allow them to converse without straining to hear each other and yet not too isolated.

He gestured for her to pick a side, then slid onto the bench across from her. Only a few feet of oilcloth-covered table separated them. They'd been much closer in the privacy of the rehab center the other night, but somehow this felt more intimate. More like a date. Which it wasn't—not even close. He was taking pity on her, not wooing her.

But it still was the closest she'd come to a social life since moving back to Paradise. And date or not, she'd be crazy not to enjoy having dinner with a good-looking man. And good-looking barely began to describe the level of hotness that was Dylan Turner. In a crisp, sea-green button-down shirt and khaki slacks, he was dressed more formally than the majority of patrons. Heck, he was more dressed up than most of the island, not counting Sunday services at All Saints' Church. But somehow he didn't seem out of place amongst the more casual shorts-and-T-shirt crowd. His laid-back attitude and general confidence made it impossible for him to look anything but comfortable in his own skin. She had no doubt he could handle whatever came his way.

Her own cotton skirt was hardly dressy, but she was glad she'd made the effort to put on something other than jeans.

"You look really nice. The skirt suits you."

Sam smoothed a hand over the material, uncomfortable with how closely he'd read her thoughts. "Thanks. I'm not sure when the last time I wore one was." She reached for one of the plastic-coated menus propped up by the salt and pepper shakers, needing something to do with her hands.

"A tomboy, huh?"

"Not exactly. At least, I didn't use to be." Back when her mother was alive, they'd had fun shopping for pretty things together. She shook the memory off, forcing herself back to the here and now. "But when you spend all your time trying to fit in as one of the guys, it's easy to forget you aren't one."

His cool blue eyes scanned up and down her body, heating her skin. "No offense, but I don't think you're ever going to be mistaken for one of the guys."

"Thanks, I think."

"No, thank you, for agreeing to dinner. If you hadn't, I'd be heating a frozen dinner instead of ordering shrimp tacos and key lime pie."

"That does sound tragic." Scanning the menu was like rereading a love letter from long ago that evoked equal parts nostalgia and longing. "I'm glad to see they kept a lot of the old favorites, but there are some new options here that look good, too. I think I could eat here every night for the rest of my life and not get tired of it."

"Have you been here since you moved back?"

She shook her head, her gaze flicking back and forth between the various options. "Oh, wow, lobster and Brie grilled cheese? I used to always order the grouper sandwich, but I don't think I can turn down something as decadent as Brie and lobster."

"So get it. As hard as you work, you deserve something wonderful."

Sam swallowed hard before daring to look up at him. His smile was easy, his body language sincere. He seemed to have offered the compliment without thought, as if it was nothing. When was the last time someone had done that? "Thanks. I think I will."

As if in response to her decision, a waitress appeared at her elbow, gray-streaked hair pulled back in a ponytail and a tired smile on her lips. "Have y'all had time to decide?"

"I think so, but you know me, I always get the same thing." Dylan returned the waitress's smile with his own hundred-watt version. "Sally, I'd like you to meet Sam Finley. She used to live here, and is back in town, working with the Fish and Wildlife Commission."

Sally turned to Sam, her green eyes widening. "That's why you looked so familiar! You're Tom Finley's little girl!"

Dylan watched Sam blink in surprise, obviously trying to place the middle-aged waitress in her memory.

"I can't believe you remember me...from back then, I mean. I've been gone so much..."

"Well, sure, I heard you were away at some fancy

school or something, but you're still an islander, and I know everyone on the island."

"Thanks. I guess I wasn't sure anyone still thought of me that way."

The older woman's expression softened. "Of course we do. People were real fond of your family. It was tragic what happened to your mother. Maybe we should have done more to help afterward. But your father—"

"He wasn't very good at accepting help," Sam finished for her.

"Well, yeah, he was just very independent."

Sam's mouth tightened. "He still is. I guess you don't see him in here much"

"Not in years, honey. But I'm sure glad you're here. Good to see how nicely you've grown up. And following in your daddy's footsteps as a wildlife officer—he must be very proud of you."

Sam nodded politely, but he could see the tension in her shoulders, tension hadn't been there before. Wanting to shift the focus to something more palatable, he tapped her menu. "Still want the lobster grilled cheese?"

Her smile returned. "Definitely. With a bowl of the conch chowder."

Sally scribbled on her pad. "Anything else? An appetizer, maybe?"

Chewing her lip, Sam scrutinized the menu. "Are the conch fritters as good as I remember?"

Sally winked. "Better."

Dylan took the menu from her and returned it to the side of the table. "Well, then, by all means, bring the lady some conch fritters."

"I'll get the order in right away. And Sam, it's good to have you back in town."

"Thanks, Sally. It's good to be back."

Sally headed to the kitchen, leaving them alone again.

"There. That wasn't so bad, was it?"

Sam shrugged. "No, but she remembers me. That helped."

"I think you are going to find a lot more people remember you than you think."

A hint of worry furrowed her brow. "If so, then why doesn't anyone else mention it?"

"Did you ever think they might be waiting for you to say something? You're the one that left—maybe they think you're too good for them now."

"That's crazy. I'm the same person I always was."

"You grew up into a beautiful woman. That can be intimidating to some people. And for all they know, you liked the girls at your fancy prep school better than the people here."

She shook her head, her dark hair mussing with the movement. "No way. I hated being away from here. And I never fit in at St. Anne's. I was too shy, from the wrong place, with the wrong accent. I was the odd girl out, complete with mousy hair and thick glasses."

He reached out and smoothed a strand of hair back behind her ear. Soft as silk, just as he'd imagined. "Well, I have a hard time believing that, but if you ever were an ugly duckling you're certainly not now. Although I would like to see you in those glasses sometime."

"So you can tease me, too?"

"Let's just say I like the sexy librarian look."

Sam's mouth opened, then closed, her cheeks flushing at his innuendo. She really was as innocent as she seemed if something that mild could embarrass her. It was refreshing to know he could make a woman blush.

But also a reminder to watch his step. He wanted to get to know her better, not scare her off. Luckily, Sally chose that moment to return with a plastic basket heaped with piping hot fritters, defusing the tension with the scent of fried food.

"Here you go, but be careful. They're a bit hot."

Sam was already reaching for one, nodding at the warning. "Thanks, I remember." She took a bite and then immediately dropped the steaming fritter into her lap. "Ouch!"

Dylan handed her a napkin from the dispenser on the edge of the table. "She did warn you."

Sam brushed the crumbs off of her shirt and shook her head. "I thought she meant spicy hot, not hot-hot."

"It seems in this case they're both." He nudged one of the glasses of ice water the waitress had left toward Sam. "Here, drink this. It will help."

She nodded and gulped down a few big swallows. "Better, thanks."

"Good." He broke open one of the steaming fritters and handed her half. "They cool faster this way. "

"Now you tell me. Where were you a minute ago?"

Fantasizing about you in nothing but a pair of glasses probably wasn't the right answer, so he just shrugged and bit into the rapidly cooling appetizer. The slightly sweet and chewy conch contrasted perfectly with the spicy peppers and crisp batter. "Do you know, there are people who have never had a conch fritter?"

She shook her head in mock sympathy. "It's a tragedy, really."

"It is. I guess they don't know what they're missing. But still, life can't quite be complete if you don't have good seafood."

A wistful look shadowed her face. "There's a lot to be thankful for in Paradise."

Dylan wanted to punch himself. She'd lived most of her life away from this, and it was obvious she'd missed out on a lot more than seafood while she was gone. He couldn't give her that time back or fix everything that had gone wrong for her, but he could at least try to keep his foot out of his mouth and make her return as welcome as possible.

And if easing her reentry into her old hometown meant spending more time with her, well, that was just an added bonus.

Chapter Five

When the waitress returned with their entrées, Sam forced herself to focus on the meal, refusing to let herself be dragged down by bad memories. Sure, she'd had a rough childhood in some ways, but she was incredibly lucky in others. And right here, right now, she was having a delicious meal in one of the most beautiful places in the world. Even better, she was having a great time. Not only had Dylan turned out to be an excellent dinner companion, but she'd actually met someone who remembered her! It was almost pathetic how much a waitress's simple comment could affect her mood, but knowing that someone remembered her mother, remembered them as a family, meant more than she had expected.

Her mom had been gone so long, and her father had changed so much, it was hard to believe any of it had been real. Sometimes she wondered if she'd imagined how good her life had been back then. Talking to someone who knew her then reassured her it wasn't all in her head. They *had* been happy, and damn it, she was going to be happy again. She was going to make friends, kick butt at her job and make her boss and her father proud of her.

"Is your sandwich okay? You've been awful quiet."

"Oh, yes. It's delicious, actually." And it was, the creamy Brie and buttery lobster a match made in heaven. "I was just thinking."

"About?" Dylan took a bite of his taco and looked expectantly at her.

"The past, the future, that sort of thing."

He nodded. "Being near the ocean can bring out some big thoughts. Something about the timelessness of the waves maybe. Whenever I get too caught up in the day-to-day grind, I hit the beach. A few hours on my board helps me back up and see the forest for the trees."

"I knew it! You are a surfer."

"Guilty as charged. I don't get as much time on the waves as I'd like, but it's one of the reasons I took the job here. I was dying to get back in the water."

She dipped a corner of her sandwich in the spicy chowder and considered that. "So where were you before you came here?"

"Boston. Which, although technically isn't far from the ocean, to find waves you have to be willing to drive a while. Which my school schedule didn't leave a lot of time for."

"Wait, you were in school in Boston?" She tried hard to picture his sun-bleached hair and laid-back attitude fitting in in New England, and failed.

"Yeah, grad school. I got an MBA, which looks good

on paper but taught me very little about bottle-feeding deer. That's all on-the-job training."

He had an MBA? "What school?"

"I did my undergrad at UF, but the MBA is from Harvard."

"You have an MBA from Harvard. And you work for a tiny nonprofit where you have to nail shingles and feed deer?" Was he crazy?

"I do more than that, but yes. I had job offers from larger companies, but I wasn't interested in the whole corporate thing. I like it here, and I'm close enough to home to visit my family when I want to. And when I get free time, which isn't very often, I admit, I can surf or just walk on the beach. Boston's a great place, but I'm a Florida boy at heart."

So not just good-looking, but smart. Smart enough to get into Harvard, and confident enough to turn down what were undoubtedly better-paying and more impressive jobs in order to have the lifestyle he preferred. She wanted to understand more about how he'd ended up following such an unconventional path, but if he didn't want to talk about it she wouldn't pry. Having her own off-limits subjects, she knew that simple questions could sometimes lead to painful answers.

Instead, she leaned back in her chair and steered the conversation to a more mundane topic. "You said your parents live nearby—does that mean you're a Florida native?"

He gave a slow, easy smile and her heart thumped a bit harder. "Yes, ma'am. My parents have a cattle ranch over on the mainland in unincorporated Palmetto County. My brother and sister both still live there, and help run the place."

"And you didn't want to stay and be part of the family business?"

"No, but it took me a while to figure that out. I majored in Agricultural Science at UF, but the closer I got to graduating, the more I wanted to do something else. I didn't tell my parents I was applying to grad school until after I got accepted. I figured they couldn't argue with a scholarship to Harvard."

So not only did he get into Harvard, he'd gotten a scholarship. Wow. "So your version of rebellion was to go get a business degree at an Ivy League school?"

He chuckled. "If you put it that way, I guess so. Not much of a rebellion, huh?"

"Hey, going against the expectations of your family is hard, no matter what."

"Is that how you ended up as a wildlife officer, because your father expected it?"

Sam sputtered, nearly choking on a sip of tea. "No, definitely not. He thought I should be a librarian or an English teacher. Joining the Fish and Wildlife Commission was the last thing he wanted for me. He thinks law enforcement isn't a suitable career for a woman. Or at least, not for his daughter. Camping out, hiking—those are fine if they're just a hobby. But chasing poachers in the back country, carrying a gun—that's way too dangerous. "

A slow, sexy smile spread over Dylan's face. "Well, then, I guess that makes us a pair of rebels, doesn't it?"

Dylan watched her shrug off his question. "I guess so, although rebelling really wasn't the goal. And I do like books, so he wasn't too far off with the librarian idea."

"But...?" There was obviously more, something she wasn't saying.

"But I wanted something that we could share, something to bring us together. And I wanted to make a difference, the way that he did."

And she wanted to make him proud.

Something inside his chest ached at the thought of this gutsy woman trying so hard to earn her own father's approval. No wonder she was determined to make things work for her in Paradise. She wasn't just trying to impress her boss or renew old friendships; she was trying to win her father's love.

"Is everyone all done?" Sally was back, ready to clear their plates.

Sam nodded. "I'm finished. How about you, Dylan?"

"Yes, thank you, Sally. And could you bring out two slices of the key lime pie, please?" He looked back to Sam. "Unless you'd prefer something else."

"Key lime pie sounds perfect."

Sally took their plates and smiled her approval. "Y'all sit tight. I'll be back with that pie in just a minute."

True to her word, she returned with the sweet, creamy dessert in record time, and he still hadn't figured out a way to ask Sam more about her relationship with her father. Maybe it was best to work up to that and start with something simpler. "So, what kinds of things are you looking forward to, now that you're back?"

She halted the fork that was halfway to her mouth. "What do you mean?"

"I mean, what are you planning as far as fun? Places you've missed, people you want to see, that kind of thing."

"Other than eating conch fritters and key lime pie?"

"Yes, other than that. Although it's not a bad start."

She licked a bit of pie from her fork, sending his blood rushing south as she appeared to consider the question.

"I don't really know. I've been pretty focused on the things I have to do, not the things I want to do. Business before pleasure, and all of that."

"That can be a pretty boring way to live."

She pursed her lips, then shook her head. "Maybe, but it's a strategy that's worked pretty well so far. It got me to where I am, and that wasn't easy." She smirked. "You aren't the only one that got a scholarship, you know. Although mine was just undergrad, and nothing as fancy as Harvard."

"So brains and looks, my favorite combination." He watched with satisfaction as her cheeks turned pink. Making her blush was becoming a bit of an addiction. Truthfully, everything about her made him want more. More time with her, but also more *for* her. She was smart, pretty and had a quick wit, but he had a feeling she'd locked most of that away in her pursuit of success. Maybe it was just his contrary nature surfacing, but he was itching to show her how much more there was to life, or could be.

"Flattery will get you nowhere."

"You know, people always say that, but in my experience a little flattery never hurts."

She shook her head in annoyance, but there was a twinkle in her eye. She wasn't totally immune to his charms; there was still hope. For what, he wasn't quite sure, but he certainly was going to stick around and find out. Maybe this was his chance. "Well, tonight's been fun, right?"

She nodded. "Actually, yes, it has."

"Don't sound so surprised."

"Hey, I'm just being honest. I wasn't sure this was a good idea, but I've had fun." She looked out over the water, her eyes seeing something he couldn't. "It's been a long time since I've just sat and relaxed. Good view, good food, perfect weather—"

"—fantastic company. Can't forget the fantastic company."

She laughed and his skin tingled in response. "Fine, yes, the company was good, too. It's been a nice night. Thank you for suggesting it. I'm just sorry your friend Dani couldn't make it."

"Yeah, me, too." Not really. "But since you've had such a good time, why don't we make plans to get together again?"

Sam bit her bottom lip, tension sharpening the crease between her brows. "Like a date?"

"That's the idea, yeah. We're both adults, and I'd like to see you again."

"Oh." She smiled, but this time it looked forced. "I don't think so. Tonight was nice, but I'm not looking to date anyone right now. I need to focus on work and on making new friends. It just isn't a good time for anything beyond that."

"You're sure? I can't bribe you with another crazy sandwich or something?"

"I'm sure. But thank you. It's been a while since a guy asked me out. I'm flattered."

What kind of blind, clueless men had she been around? "Well, the offer stands. Maybe once you get your feet under you, and things settle down…"

"Maybe."

Damn. It had been a long time since he'd been shot

down, longer still since it had really mattered. Actually, it had been quite a while since he'd even asked a woman out, although plenty of the eligible ladies in Paradise had made it clear they were interested. He'd just been too busy trying to keep the wildlife sanctuary afloat. Maybe he was getting as bad as he accused her of being, all work and no play.

He'd have to rectify that, and soon. But somehow the idea didn't spark much enthusiasm. Not when the woman he really wanted to go out with was sitting right in front of him, and she'd turned him down flat.

Sam fiddled with her fork, pushing the last bit of her pie around her plate. Injured animals, lawbreakers, outboard motors that refused to start: all of those she could handle with confidence. So why did a man asking her out make her want to run home and hide?

She'd been asked out before—not often—but it had happened. She'd never had a problem turning anyone down. And men in general certainly didn't make her nervous. She worked in a male-dominated field; she knew how to handle herself. So why was her pulse pounding louder than the surf crashing on the rocks below?

Because this time, she hadn't wanted to say no.

And that was terrifying.

Until now, she'd parroted the line about needing to focus on her work or school as an excuse. But now that she was finally interested in a guy it was actually true. She really couldn't divert time into figuring out a relationship, not now. Maybe if she was the kind of girl who could keep things casual it would work, but despite her lack of experience she was pretty sure she wasn't a casual kind of person—not when it came to relationships.

Her inability to deal with her father's distance had taught her that.

Picking up on her discomfort, Dylan shrugged, as if it was all no big deal. To him it probably wasn't. "Well, maybe when you get settled, you can look me up. In the meantime, let me know if you get any leads on those poachers."

"Poachers?" Her mind struggled to switch gears. "I mean, sure I will, although it doesn't look too promising right now." One dinner with a handsome guy and she'd already forgotten about work. Obviously, turning him down was the right decision. She couldn't afford any confusion when it came to protecting the wildlife of Paradise Isle. "What will you do with the deer?"

"Oh, we'll keep him for a little while, until he can fend for himself. It won't take too long. He's doing well, thanks to us finding him in time."

"You're the one that found him."

"And you found me." Dylan cleared his throat. "Anyway, if you'd like to check on him, you can stop by anytime."

"Thanks, maybe I will." Probably not, though. As much as she'd like to see the fawn's progress with her own eyes, she didn't want to risk giving Dylan the wrong idea. Better to end things now, before it got awkward. She'd hoped he might be able to help her make some friends, but given the circumstances she'd be better off without him.. Better to fumble her way through on her own than get in over her head with him.

Sally approached the table. "Anyone want coffee? Decaf?"

"No, thanks." It was time to leave, no matter how much fun she was having. Time to face reality, and sadly reality didn't often feature Brie and lobster with a gorgeous guy. More like paperwork and peanut butter and jelly. "I'll take the check, though."

Dylan's gaze shot to her in surprise. "I don't think so. Dinner's on me."

"But this was about helping me out, so I should pay." Letting him pay would make it a date.

"First, it was supposed to be a chance for me to introduce you to a potential ally, but since she didn't come I didn't do anything to help you. Second, you paid for the pizza you shared with me the other night, so I already owe you a meal. Third, my mother would have me fed to the gators if she heard I'd asked a woman to dinner and then let her pay."

"But—"

"No arguments." He took the check from Sally, who was openly amused at their back-and-forth bickering. "I may be a rebel, but I'm still afraid of my mama."

Sally nodded in approval, taking the check and the cash he handed her. "The man has a point."

"Fine, I know when I'm outnumbered. But I'm only agreeing because I paid for the pizza last time." That she could justify to herself.

"Whatever works." He winked, then stood. "I'll walk you to your car, unless you'd like to take a stroll on the beach first. It's turning into a beautiful night."

She glanced down at the shoreline, where the last gasp of daylight was being taken over by night as the moon rose over the water. It was gorgeous, but Dylan had been hard enough to deal with in a crowded restaurant. No way was she going on a romantic walk with him, not after he'd already asked her out. Standing up, she slung her purse over her shoulder. "I really need to get home. My cat will be waiting for me."

Could she be any more pathetic? Her *cat* was waiting for her? She'd already admitted to struggling to fit in to her old hometown; now he'd think she was a hermit. Or at least in the early stages of becoming a crazy cat lady.

"A cat person, huh?"

He'd kept a straight face, she'd give him that. "Yes, actually. I like dogs, too, but I work long hours, so a cat makes more sense."

He motioned for her to go first, and walked with her across the deck toward the stairs to the parking lot. "I'm a dog guy myself. I've been thinking of adopting one for a while. I could bring it to work with me, so that's not an issue."

"Well, why haven't you, then?"

He shrugged, stopping as they neared her car. "I don't know. I guess the right one hasn't come along yet. When it does, I'll know."

"I guess." She opened the door to her truck and slid in, thinking how if she wanted to adopt a dog she'd research breeds, make a list of traits she was looking for and scour the shelters until she found one. But it was very clear that Dylan had his own way of doing things. "Seems like it would be faster to just go look for one."

"Well, I figure some things you can't rush. But when it's right, it's worth the wait."

Chapter Six

"Damn it!" Dylan jerked his shirt, now soaked with scalding hot coffee, away from his skin.

"Bad day, surfer boy?" Dani Post walked up to where he stood at the counter of The Grind and handed him a stack of napkins, a smirk on her face.

"Where did you come from?" He hadn't seen her when he'd come in the coffee shop a minute ago. Of course he'd been more focused on his need for caffeine than his surroundings. "And no, I'm not having a bad day, I just spilled my coffee. I must have put the lid on wrong, that's all."

She tilted her head, her gaze missing nothing as she considered. He hated when she used her lawyer look on him. Crap, maybe he *was* in a bad mood, if Dani could get on his nerves this quickly.

"You look like crap. My guess is you were in a funk before the coffee issue."

Or maybe she was just annoying.

"Let me guess, your friend from last night found out I wasn't coming and stood you up?"

He replaced the lid on the now half-empty cup of coffee, carefully this time, and took a large swallow before answering. Thankfully, The Grind made their coffee as strong as it was hot. "No, counselor, she didn't stand me up. As a matter of fact we had a very nice dinner. Without you."

"Uh-huh." She sipped her own drink, eyeing him over the brim. "So then why are you here, with circles under your eyes, instead of in the office?"

"Because it's Saturday?"

"Which would make sense if you ever took weekends off. But you don't. You've been working seven days a week since I met you. So again, what's up?"

She had him there. Spying an empty table outside, he headed for it, not surprised when she followed and sat down with him. A typical lawyer, she wasn't going to end an interrogation midstream. "I didn't sleep well, so I thought I'd get some decent coffee before heading in. Nothing more than that."

"You have coffee at home. And at the wildlife center."

"I said *decent* coffee."

"Okay, I'll give you that. This is definitely better than the stuff you served me at the last board meeting." Not to be deterred, she switched tactics. "So why didn't you sleep well?" When he simply glared, she tipped up her cup and waited. She was a good friend, but she had the persistence of a pit bull. If he didn't give her something, she'd keep on him, but he wasn't about to admit he'd been up half the night thinking about Sam. "I just had things on my mind."

"Things, or a person?" At his startled look, she laughed. "Don't worry, I'm not a mind reader. But you know how fast gossip gets around in this town. I hear you were all gaga-eyed over a certain wildlife officer last night."

Well, hell. "Sally?"

She shrugged, and gestured to the crowds of people strolling around Main Street. "Probably, plus anyone else with two eyes and a mouth. By now half the people in town know, if not more. I heard it from my mom when I stopped by there this morning to pick up some papers. And she heard it from Mrs. Rosenberg, I think. You're the town's most eligible bachelor, and this is the first time you've been spotted out on a date in months. That's big news in a place this small."

"It wasn't a date."

"You bought a pretty woman dinner on a Friday night. Of course people thought it was a date."

The headache that had been threatening all morning ratcheted up a notch. "You think the gossip has gotten back to Sam yet?"

"Maybe. Depends who she talks to. Sometimes people are less likely to bring it up with the person that the gossip is about."

"Obviously you have no such compunction."

"I'm your friend. It's my job to get the straight scoop. I had planned to stop by the wildlife center to quiz you. It was just luck that I bumped in to you here first."

"You already knew what you wanted to ask, so that bit about me looking like hell—"

"Was true. You look exhausted." She leaned in, resting her elbows on the table. "I was just going to tease you about finally having a night out. I didn't know you were actually hung up on her. This is way better than I thought."

"Nice. And for the record, I'm not hung up on her. We had dinner, that's it."

"So you didn't ask her out again?"

No point in denying it; obviously his fellow diners had done more than their share of eavesdropping. "Yes, I did. But I'm guessing you knew that, too."

"I did. What I didn't know was that she shot you down. That I figured out all on my own, from your less than pleasant attitude." Dani shook her head in mock sorrow. "I never thought I'd see it happen. Half the women on the island are dying to go out with you, and you find the one that isn't interested."

"I don't see how this is at all funny. Or even your business, for that matter."

"Hey, don't shoot the messenger. I figured you'd want a heads-up, but maybe I should let you brood in peace."

"Yeah, maybe." Rationally, none of this was Dani's fault. Other than her standing him up last night, but he'd been happy enough when she'd canceled. Still, he wasn't in the mood to talk about it. He didn't even want to think about it. Getting turned down was a bruise to his ego, but not a big deal in the scheme of things. At least, it shouldn't have been. That it obviously *was* just made things worse. And now he knew everyone in town was talking about it.

Although at least, from what Dani said, the part about Sam turning him down hadn't hit the gossip circuit. Yet.

"Hey, Dani?"

She stopped, coffee in one hand, designer purse in the other.

"Thanks for letting me know."

"Any time. And don't worry, I won't tell anyone she turned you down—I'll let her do that."

Sam had woken up early, thanks to a very loud, very insistent cat who firmly believed breakfast was the most important meal of the day. She had poured kibble for him and cereal for herself, then given the apartment a quick cleaning like she did every Saturday morning. Normally she'd spend an hour or two catching up on paperwork after that, but today she was feeling...restless. Maybe because the weather was so nice. The humidity of summer had finally started to dissipate and there was a cool breeze coming through her open windows. Or maybe Dylan's comment about her being all work and no play had hit a nerve. Either way, the thought of spending the morning at her desk held less appeal than usual.

Grabbing her keys and a tote bag, she figured she'd start by returning her library books. She could pick up a few novels and then hit the grocery store and get her weekly shopping done. Not exactly a raucous good time, but better than sitting here working. At least she'd be out of the house.

Traffic was light; as on most weekends, more people could be found strolling the sidewalk than driving. Lighthouse Avenue was bustling, full of parents pushing strollers, teenagers windowshopping, and seniors dallying over coffee at outdoor café tables. She'd missed living in a place where people waved when they saw you, and no one was ever in too big of a hurry to say good morning or ask you how you were.

The library was busy as well, with a preschool story hour going on in one corner and a sign advertising an Internet for Seniors class in the community room upstairs.

Still, it was a haven. Even the smells of old books and printer ink reminded her of the many hours she'd spent here happily lost in a book.

"Looking for anything in particular?" Mrs. Grey, the librarian, asked as Sam emptied her tote bag of books into the return slot. "There's a few romantic suspense books in the new release section I think you might like."

"Thanks, I'll take a look." Mrs. Grey had been watching out for her for years, ever since she'd found her crying in the stacks at ten years old. Only a few weeks after her mom's death, she'd been looking for somewhere to hide from prying eyes. Without saying a word, the no-nonsense librarian had handed her a tissue and put her to work as a volunteer. Having something to do had kept her mind off her grief, but it was the books themselves that had made the biggest difference. She'd devoured every happily-ever-after she could find, starting with fairy tales and working her way up to Jane Austen. Now she was a confirmed romance fan, and Mrs. Grey always had a few to recommend whenever Sam was in town.

Waving goodbye, Sam quickly refilled her bag with new reading material, including ones the librarian had recommended. Once checked out, she loaded the books into her trunk and drove to the island's only grocery store, located at the edge of town where picturesque mom-and-pop shops gave way to the few chain stores.

Grabbing a cart from the corral out front, she mentally recited her grocery list. Milk, eggs, coffee, fruit, bread and more frozen dinners. Oh, and cat food. Cheesy would mutiny if she forgot his special canned food.

As she zipped up and down the aisles, she tossed in items from her list. And a few things that weren't on the list. First, her favorite chocolate bar because it was on sale, and then carrots because she felt guilty about the chocolate. Veggies canceled out sugar, right? All that was left was the frozen dinners. She was debating between ravioli with meat sauce and orange chicken when someone stopped beside her. "Sorry, I'll be out of your way in a minute."

"No hurry. You're Sam, right? Sam Finley?"

Sam turned, orange chicken in hand, and tried to place the woman. Tall, with brunette hair cut in a sleek bob, she had a basket with a single pint of ice cream, and didn't look at all familiar.

"Yes. Have we met?"

"No, but we were supposed to."

"I'm...sorry?" What on earth? She racked her mind for some missed appointment or ditched social event.

"Oh, no, don't be. I'm the one that ditched you."

"You did?"

"Last night, at dinner?"

"Oh! You must be Dylan's friend, the one who had to babysit."

"That's me. Sorry, I should have said that up front." She held out an impeccably manicured hand. "I'm Dani Post, local public defender, babysitter extraordinaire and your biggest fan."

Okay, this was getting weird. "Care to explain that last part?"

"I heard that you turned Dylan down for a date. I've been dying for someone to do that. He's a great guy, but his ego needed to be knocked down a peg."

Sam laughed as she tossed in a few more frozen meals. "He does seem rather confident."

Dani pulled her cart alongside Sam's. "Oh, he's totally full of himself. And what's worse, I can't blame him—

he's too good-looking and smart to be humble. But as his friend I can say that a bit of a reality check isn't going to hurt him any."

"I doubt me turning him down had much of an effect, but thanks, I think." She smiled. "I've got to check out before my food melts, but it was nice to meet you, Dani." And it was. Something about the brash lawyer's forwardness appealed to her.

"Oh, I'm checking out, too." When Sam glanced down again at the single item in Dani's basket, she shrugged. "I had a rough week, and ice cream is how I handle stress."

"Fair enough." She started to empty her own purchases onto the checkout counter, only to be frozen by an ear-piercing squeal from the cashier.

"Eek! I was hoping you'd come to my register! You're Dylan Turner's new girlfriend, right?"

Before she could utter a word in protest, the gum-chewing teen was calling to the cashier at the next station. "Denise! Get over here!" Turning back to Sam, she batted mascara-coated lashes in rhythm with her gum-popping jaws. "So, is he as sexy as he seems? I bet he's an amazing kisser."

Joining her friend, the other cashier squeezed into the small space. "Are you going out again tonight? Do you think you'll move in with him?"

Sam stood frozen, like a deer caught in headlights. "No. I mean… I'm not—"

"Olivia, didn't I see you giving Jacob Langley a ride last night? Is your mother letting you date him again?" Dani had moved up next to Sam, and was standing, hands on her hips, staring down the chattering teen.

Eyes wide, the girl turned her focus from Sam to Dani. "You're not going to tell her, are you, Ms. Post? I was just helping him out. We're not back together—really, his parents aren't letting him date at all right now."

"Well, I know gossip can get out of hand quickly, so if you're sure there's nothing going on..."

The girl nodded, her hoop earrings swaying with the motion. "I'm sure."

The other cashier, apparently not wanting to get in the middle of whatever was going on, returned to her station, leaving the now much more subdued Olivia, who quickly checked Sam and then Dani out.

Once outside, Sam stopped and turned to Dani, blocking her path with the cart. "What on earth was that?"

"That was the town gossip mill at full steam. Or at least the younger generation's version of it. The downside to small-town living, I'm afraid."

Sam's head spun. "So you're saying everyone is going to be talking about me like that?"

"Probably. For now, anyway. Dylan's a hot topic all on his own, and since you were out with him, that makes you fair game. Generally people are a lot more circumspect when it comes to these things, but Olivia's young and a bit impulsive."

"And what was that about seeing her with some guy?"

"Jacob. He was her boyfriend until he got busted for underage drinking and her mom made her stop seeing him. I wasn't his public defender—a friend was—but I know he got community service and some substance abuse counseling. As for last night, there were actually several kids in the car. It didn't look romantic at all. But I thought it might be good for her to get a taste of what gossip can feel like from the other side."

"Well, it worked, thank you. I'm not exactly comfortable being the center of attention, as I'm sure you noticed. Honestly, I think I might need some ice cream now."

"Lucky for you, I've got enough Rocky Road for the two of us."

Sam unpacked the last of her groceries, still not sure how she'd ended up inviting Dani back to her apartment. Or rather why she'd gone along when Dani had invited herself over. Her new friend had argued that since Sam had groceries that needed to be put away, and Dani had nothing planned other than a dessert binge, it just made sense for her to tag along back to Sam's place.

Which was why there were now two bowls of Rocky Road on the table instead of the single peanut butter and jelly sandwich she'd planned for herself. Not that she had wanted to say no, but she was struck by the feeling that she'd never really had a choice in the matter. Dani Post was a force of nature; Sam could only imagine what it must be like to face her down in a courtroom.

"If you don't get over here soon, your ice cream is going to melt."

Sam grabbed the bowl and leaned against the counter, savoring her first bite of the creamy sweetness. "I actually kind of like it when it gets all soft. When I was a kid, I called it ice-cream soup."

Dani made a face in mock horror. "Ugh, my sister did that, too. I never understood it—the whole point of ice cream is that it's cold. But in the spirit of new friendship I'm willing to overlook what is obviously a serious character flaw."

"In the spirit of new friendship, or because you want more details about my dinner with Dylan?"

"Trust me, I already got the details from Dylan. And

what he didn't tell me, my mother and half the town will fill me in on. What I want to know is, what are you going to do now?"

Sam swallowed hard, the cold treat making a lump in her throat. "What do you mean? I told Dylan I need to focus on my career right now, and that's exactly what I'm going to do."

Dani nodded. "Right, but from what I understand, your biggest problem there is forging the kind of connections that will bring in leads. And that kind of social networking isn't something you can force."

"Well, I'm going to have to figure out a way to speed up the process. If I can't show my boss that I'm earning the trust of the citizens, I'm going to end up riding a desk somewhere with more paperwork than people." Just like her father. The difference was that he hadn't been forced into it, he'd just given up—on the job and on life in general. She knew it was his way of dealing with grief, but she still couldn't understand it. Not when she was one of the people he'd given up on.

"And that doesn't leave room for dating Dylan, huh?"

"Afraid not." No matter how hot he was.

"What about just a fling then?" She waggled her eyebrows. "Maybe just to ease the tension, if you know what I mean?"

She felt her cheeks heat. "I'm not really the fling type."

"Serious relationship kind of girl, huh? Is there a guy nursing a broken heart up north somewhere?"

As if. "No, no old boyfriend. Like I said, my career is my focus."

Dani's gazed locked on her, the lawyer mode clearly in play. "Wait, no recent old boyfriend, or no old boyfriends at all?"

Damn. Ducking her head, she put more effort into washing their bowls than was strictly necessary. "I had a few dates here and there." Bad ones. "But no real relationships, no. I was too busy studying, and then I was at the academy. And anyway, Cheesy is more than enough responsibility right now, aren't you, boy?"

The big orange cat, stretched out in a beam of sunshine on the kitchen floor, twitched an ear and went back to grooming himself.

"Hey, I get it. Law school wasn't exactly relationship friendly. But at some point you have to take a risk and put yourself out there, you know?"

"Risk" was so not her favorite word. "Maybe. But now isn't the time." Not when she had so much else on the line. She couldn't chance losing her job *and* her heart.

Dani didn't look convinced, but at least she was perceptive enough to know when to back off. "All right, then let's figure out how to save your job, and then we'll worry about your love life." Reaching into her oversize handbag, she whipped out a yellow legal pad and a pen. "Let's start by making a list of people you used to know, people that would remember you, and go from there."

One hour and several cups of coffee later, Sam was ready to declare defeat. She'd remembered more people than she'd expected, but most of them had moved off the island. She planned to contact the few that remained, but most of them were from her father's generation and may have less than favorable memories, considering his abrupt withdrawal from Paradise society after her mother's death. Sally at the restaurant had been understanding, but there were sure to be at least some hard feelings about the way he'd left things.

On the bright side, she was starting with a mostly

clean slate, other than those few. But that also meant she'd need even more time to make inroads, time she didn't have.

Getting up, she stretched and headed to the kitchen. "Want more coffee? Or a sandwich or something?"

"No, I've got to get going. I've got a case to prep for tomorrow." Looking at the paper in front of her, Dani sighed. "I know you were hoping for better news, but you'll make it work. I'll introduce you to some of my friends, and we'll go from there. Or you could change your mind, and go out with Dylan."

"How on earth would that help?"

"Hello, you saw how the cashiers acted when they thought you were his girlfriend. You were practically a celebrity. You'd be on everyone's radar, and people would be clamoring to get to know you." When Sam turned back to her, she quickly added, "But of course you shouldn't go out with him under false pretenses. I was just thinking out loud. Forget I said anything."

Sam nodded, but her stomach was churning, and not just from all the sugar and caffeine. Given unlimited time, she could and would make things work in Paradise. But if she was going to establish herself here in the few weeks before the Outdoor Days Festival she needed to think outside the box. And she needed to do it quickly.

Chapter Seven

Dylan shoved a hand through his hair as he pored over the numbers in front of him. Some months, balancing the budget was a quick and easy chore, but it looked like this wasn't going to be one of them. The spreadsheet on his screen was showing an alarming amount of red, and after an hour of wrestling with numbers he was starting to think he was going to need magic, not math, to make things work. Partly because, unlike a normal business, there was no way to predict how many animals they might treat in a given time period, or what care they'd need. Add in the expense of the roof repair and he was almost ready to pack it in and move back to Boston.

Almost. But no Boston firm could offer him the kind of experiences he'd had here. He just needed a break and some coffee. Then somehow he'd get the numbers to work—he always did.

He was just filling his cup when he heard the front

door open behind him. Assuming it was one of the volunteers, he called out a greeting while stirring some sugar into the hopelessly bitter brew. "Morning."

"Good morning to you, too." Sam? Abandoning his drink, he spun around. "Hey, what are you doing here? Did you come by to see the fawn?"

She hesitated for a brief moment, then nodded. "Yes. How's he doing?"

"Really well. I checked on him this morning when I came in and he nearly knocked me over looking for his bottle. He definitely has his strength back."

"I'm so glad." Her tone was sincere, but there was still an aura of tension around her. Did she think he'd overstated things to protect her?

"Want to go see him?" Maybe she'd relax once she saw for herself that the orphan was on the road to recovery.

"Yes, please. I'd like that—if it's not too much trouble, I mean."

"Not at all. I was taking a break anyway." He gestured to his cooling coffee. "Would you like a cup?"

"No, thanks, I had some on the way here."

"Smart choice. This stuff's terrible, but trust me when I say the budget doesn't allow for better." He glared at the computer screen, still displaying its crimson figures.

She followed his gaze and grimaced. "I don't know much about accounting, but that can't be good."

"I know a whole lot about accounting, and I can assure you that it's worse than not good. But hey, that's what I signed up for."

"Bad coffee and impossible budgets?"

"More or less. But you forgot the manual labor and occasional animal poop."

"And yet you're still here."

He shrugged. "What can I say, I'm a glutton for punishment. But maybe not the best person to be giving you career advice, come to think of it."

"Please. You're doing something that you love, and where you can use your skills to make a difference. That's something to be proud of."

Again, he was blown away by how well she understood him, maybe more than he understood himself. "Thanks, I needed to hear that today. Now, let's go see that fawn."

He led her back through the treatment area to the enclosures. He'd moved the fawn to a larger one, where he had access to a fenced outdoor area. Spotting the baby deer before Dylan did, Sam half jogged the last few yards. "Look! He's eating!"

"He sure is. I've been bringing in trimmings from the bushes on my property to supplement his feed, and he can't get enough. He probably doesn't really need much in the way of bottles anymore, but the vet wants to keep him on them twice a day for a bit longer, just to put some extra weight on him before he's released."

Sam rested her forehead against the wire fencing of the cage, watching the fawn delicately strip the leaves off a branch with his long tongue. "Is there anything I can do to help with him?"

"Nah, he'll be fine. Unless you have lots of acorns on your property? If you do, you could bring him some of those. We've got the local school collecting them as treats for some of our animals, but we can always use a few more."

"Acorns, got it." She watched for another minute, then turned to him, her hands shoved in her pockets, posture stiff. "Before I go, there was something else I wanted to talk to you about."

Instinct told him this was more than a question of paperwork or protocol, but he kept his voice casual, not wanting to spook her before she got around to explaining her real reasons for coming. "Sure, what's up?"

"Well, after we had dinner the other night, it seems people started to talk. About us."

Crap, was that what she was upset about? "Listen, I'm sorry about that. I didn't think about how it would look—"

"No, it's fine. It's just that, well, somehow word got around that I'm your..." She scuffed one well-worn hiking boot in the dirt. "Well, people think I'm your girlfriend." She blushed, her cheeks turning a faint pink. "Or something."

"Ah. Well, I can try to put the word out that we're just friends, but it may take a few days for the gossip to die down. People always prefer an interesting bit of make-believe over the truth."

"Actually, I'd rather you didn't."

"No?" Her cheeks were still rosy, but she'd summoned up the same strength he'd seen on her in the field the other day. Whatever it was she wanted, she seemed determined to get it.

She shook her head, brown waves of hair shimmering in the sunlight. "My goal all along has been to meet people, and as stupid as it sounds, dating you would have people interested in getting to know me."

Where was she going with this? "Do you really think so? I mean, I know there was some gossip going around, but—"

"I was practically interrogated by two cashiers at the grocery store yesterday. I'm sure. Just being seen with you has made me a person of interest. And Dani seemed pretty sure that wasn't an isolated event."

Dani. He should have known she figured into this. "So what are you suggesting, exactly? You aren't really suggesting we date just to help your job, are you?" Part of him, mostly the area below the belt, welcomed the idea. But there was no way he could justify taking advantage of her in that way, even if she was serious. He had to have misunderstood.

"Actually, that's exactly what I'm suggesting."

Sam watched Dylan's eyes go wide and instantly realized her mistake. "Not for real, of course."

"Of course." His voice sounded a bit strangled, and Sam mentally kicked herself for screwing this up so badly. She'd planned out everything she was going to say last night, but as soon as she'd seen him she'd forgotten every word of it. And she never choked, not on a test in school, not on the firing range, not in the field. But she had today. She'd prattled on about the darned deer, and then she'd made it sound like she was willing to— well, she wasn't sure exactly what she'd made it sound like she was willing to do. Either way, she needed to get her foot out of her mouth and clarify things before she ended up looking any more pathetic.

"What I meant to say was, I'd like to make a proposition." His eyebrows shot up and she rolled her eyes. "Maybe proposition is the wrong word. An arrangement, a purely platonic arrangement."

"One that involves us dating?"

"Yes and no. One that gives the *appearance* of us dating. Basically, I would need you to go out with me a few times. Just enough to get people talking. Then instead of me trying to work my way into the community, the community will come to me."

"I can kind of see how that would work. Maybe. But what do I get out of this…arrangement?"

Darn it. She'd spent half the night trying to figure that part out, and she still didn't have an answer. "Acorns?" He'd said the animals needed those.

He tipped his head, as if considering.

"And I'll volunteer here at the wildlife center. I can clean cages, do laundry, help with fund-raising, whatever you need."

"So you're willing to work here, on top of the job you already have, and all I have to do is agree to date you?"

"Pretend to date me." She needed to make that part very clear or this was never going to work. Assuming it had any chance of working at all. "And yes, that's the deal."

"Okay."

"Really?" Could it be that easy?

"Sure, why not? We go out a few times, have some fun and I get another volunteer."

"Right, and it's just for a few weeks, until the Outdoor Days Festival. Then we can go our separate ways. As friends, of course."

"Right, as friends." He started back up the gravel path to the main building. "You're welcome to stay here with the fawn if you want, but I've got to get back to work."

She followed behind, trying not to notice how well his jeans fit. She couldn't afford to be distracted by anything right now, not even a cute butt. "Ah, yes, the budget. Anything I can do to help?"

He looked back with a smirk. "You're already providing free labor, so I'd say that's helping. And don't worry, we'll make some money at the festival, selling prints of

the animals here. Dani's sister, Mollie, is an incredible
photographer and always donates her work for the cause.
That should bring in some cash to get us through the win-
ter. Until then I'll just have to be creative."

"Well, I'm sure you'll manage." He seemed so confident in everything he did; she couldn't imagine living life
just trusting that everything would work out. She always
had to have everything planned out to the last detail, and
even then she still worried. Right now, she was mostly
concerned that she'd just bitten off more than she could
chew. Would people really believe that a guy like Dylan
was involved with a girl like her?

Shoving down the old insecurities, she trailed him
into the office and sat on the edge of the desk. Now that
he'd agreed to the plan, she wasn't quite sure how to pull
this charade off. "So, about the whole dating thing... I
was thinking we should start right away."

He leaned back in his chair. "Fine by me. How about
dinner tonight at Mary's Diner, say seven o'clock? It's
trivia night, so there should be a good crowd."

Her heart thumped. She'd been thinking in a few days,
not a few hours. And the mention of a crowd certainly
didn't calm her nerves. But in for a penny, in for a pound.
It wasn't like she had any other viable options at this
point. "Sounds great. I'll meet you there."

"If you want it to really look like a date, I should pick
you up."

"Oh, right. Okay."

He pushed a piece of paper and a pen across the desk
to her. "Write down your phone number and address,
and I'll be there a little before seven."

She quickly scribbled down the information, then
passed it to him. He ripped off a section and wrote his

own number down, then handed it over. "If you need to contact me before then, that's my cell. I pretty much always have it with me."

"Thanks." She stood, wondering if he found this whole situation anywhere near as awkward as she did. Probably not. He was already starting to focus on the work in front of him. "I'll see you tonight then. And thanks again for doing this."

"It's no big deal."

Maybe not to him, but it was to her. Proving herself to her boss was the biggest thing in her life right now. Once she knew she was staying in Paradise long term, then maybe she and her father could figure out some way to mend their rocky relationship. But that wasn't going to happen if she was demoted, or worse, fired. Her only chance to impress him was to show him that she was a success.

Failure wasn't an option.

For once Dylan was glad he was the only person stuck in the office on a Sunday. Because right now he needed some alone time to figure out what on earth he had just agreed to do.

When Sam had come looking for him, he'd started to hope she'd changed her mind about going out with him. And in the end, he'd been right. But a fake relationship? This wasn't some daytime soap opera; it was real life. And in real life people didn't have romances of convenience, or whatever the term was.

The very idea was crazy. And yet he'd said yes. And not because he needed another volunteer or her acorns. But because there was no way he was going to turn down a chance to spend more time with her.

Pathetic, but true. If she wouldn't date him for real, he'd take what he could get. Which right now meant dinner and a trivia competition with the one woman on the island who made his palms sweat and his pulse pound.

Not the worst agreement, when you looked at it that way.

Feeling a bit better, he set the alarm on his phone for six and dove back into his work.

Hours later, he had finished with the current budget crisis and started the process of applying for a new grant. He was on the third page of what seemed like a never-ending application when his phone buzzed, alerting him to the time. He'd worked straight through lunch, a bad habit, but thanks to the alarm he'd have time for a quick shower before picking Sam up. He'd started using one in college after he got so hyperfocused cramming for a test that he'd actually missed the exam he was studying for.

As he was shutting down the computer, the evening volunteer staff began to show up for the nightly feeding. "Hey, boss. You leaving?" Trish, one of the regulars, signed in on the volunteer sheet.

"Yeah, I've got dinner plans. A date, actually." Might as well start feeding the rumor mill now. "Sam Finley, the wildlife officer that just moved back to town? I'm taking her to trivia night."

Trish stopped writing to stare. "You've got a date? You never date." She blushed. "Not that you couldn't if you wanted to."

"Well, tonight I want to, and I'd better run if I'm going to be on time." Waving, he headed for the door. "Have a good night, and make sure you lock up."

The trip to his place only took a few minutes in the nonexistent Paradise traffic, leaving him just enough time to shower, shave and change before heading to Sam's place. Her apartment was on the other side of town, but nothing was very far on such a small island and he made it to her door a full ten minutes before seven.

He knocked and waited. Should he have stopped for flowers or something? It was a first date, but did the normal rules apply when the pretenses were false?

Either way, it was too late now. The door opened, and an incredibly large orange cat tried to squeeze through the opening. Dylan blocked the cat with his foot, and looked at Sam in question. "Is he allowed to go out, or is he trying to get away with something?"

She reached down and scooped the cat up before opening the door the rest of the way. "He's being a pain. He's indoors only, no matter what he tries to tell you."

Indeed, the massive cat was meowing vehemently, as if arguing his position. Dylan shut the door behind him, and then gave the big-headed tom a scratch. "Trust me, fella, you're better off in here."

Sam set the cat on the floor, then brushed at her shirt. "Well, that's just great. Now I'm covered in hair."

"It looks good on you. Besides, remember where I work—animal fur is practically an accessory there."

She gave him a skeptical look and kept picking off the orange hairs stuck to her plum V-neck T-shirt. Letting his gaze trail down, he took in her snug jeans and boots and wished again that she'd agree to date him for real.

"All right, that's as good as I can manage. Might as well get going."

"Wow. Try not to sound too enthusiastic. This was your idea, remember." He was starting to wonder if his ego would survive their little arrangement.

"I know." She grabbed a small purse off the entryway

table and slipped it over her shoulder. "But that doesn't mean I think it's a good idea. It's just the only one I could come up with."

"I'm flattered, truly."

She smiled wryly. "Sorry. It's not hanging out with you I'm worried about. It's everyone else. If yesterday's experience at the grocery store is any indication, we're going to be the main attraction tonight."

"And you don't like being in the spotlight." That went along with what he knew of her so far.

"Not at all. The idea of everyone looking at me, watching everything I say or do…" She shuddered.

"Honey, I've got news for you. It doesn't matter who you're with or where you go. People are going to be watching you. You're a beautiful woman and that attracts attention."

She rolled her eyes at him. "Somehow I doubt it. You're the reason I'm going to be center stage. I'm just riding your coattails."

"Sorry, but you're a showstopper all on your own. The only thing I'm doing is making you more approachable. A gorgeous woman by herself, that's intimidating. But if you're with me, someone they already know, they'll feel comfortable coming up and being introduced. Trust me."

With a small sigh she opened the door for them, careful to lock it after he'd followed her out. "I guess I have to, don't I?"

"No worries, Sam. I've got your back." He'd seen how vulnerable she was, despite her law-enforcement exterior, and there was no way he was going to let her get hurt again.

Chapter Eight

Mary's Diner hadn't changed at all in the decade since Sam had last been there. Actually, it probably hadn't changed since the day it opened. The fifties'-style decor was still spotlessly clean, with black-and-white checkerboard floor tiles, red booths and chrome accents that somehow looked both vintage and brand-new at the same time. Most days, people came and went quickly, usually blue-collar workers grabbing a quick bite or families getting a meal in between school and sport practices.

But Sunday night was trivia night—when the place turned into a Paradise hot spot. Singles looking to mingle and couples on dates would fill the tables and line up at the bar, everyone hoping to win the coveted top prize—a gift certificate for one of Mary's famous pies.

The contest didn't start until 8:00, but the tables were already filing up as friends shared an all-American meal before the competition. Dylan steered her to one of the few remaining booths, back near the kitchen, waving and nodding at people on the way. He seemed to know everyone, and she felt her smile growing tight by the time they sat down. Just like high school, when the popular kids ruled the school and she'd been lost and alone in a sea of faces.

Except this time she wasn't alone. Dylan was with her, sitting right across from her and looking like he'd stepped out a surfer magazine in his tight T-shirt and Bermuda shorts. She might feel out of place, but he was in his element. She just had to trust that he would keep up his end of the bargain.

"Hey, Dylan! Who's your friend?"

"Hi, Lynne. This is Sam Finley. She grew up here and just moved back." He turned to Sam, then back to the waitress. "Sam, this is Lynne. She moved here a few years ago."

"Hi, Lynne." Sam accepted a menu, sizing up the other woman. Mid to late twenties, pretty blond hair in a loose braid, blue eyes that sparkled with curiosity. "Nice to meet you."

"Nice to meet you, Sam. What brings you back to Paradise?"

"I signed on with the FWC, and when they had an opening here I jumped on it. Nowhere else has ever felt like home, you know?"

She smiled. "I think I do. When my mom moved here, I thought she was crazy to pick such a small town to retire in. But last year I came and stayed with her after she broke her foot, and the place grew on me. I was only supposed to stay a few weeks and it's been almost two years. Now I can't imagine living anywhere else. But... enough about me. How did you two meet?"

"Sam found one of the orphaned fawns we've got over at the wildlife sanctuary." He reached across the table and laid a hand on hers, sending tingles of awareness up her arm. "It seems I can't resist a lady in uniform."

Pulling her hand back, Sam handed her menu back to the waitress. "Actually, we both found the deer." She appreciated Dylan giving her the credit, but she preferred to stick with the truth. False relationships notwithstanding. "In fact, for a few minutes, I thought Dylan might be a poacher."

Dylan gave a wry smile. "It's true. Thankfully, not only did I talk her out of arresting me, but I even got her to agree to a date."

Sam bit her tongue. This was what she'd asked him to do, and if the look of delight on Lynne's face could be trusted it was working.

"What a great story! It's like something out of a romance novel."

Hardly. But Dylan kicked her under the table, prompting her to reply. "Um, yeah, I guess it is." She forced a smile. She hated lying, but if she was going to do it, she had better make it believable.

"So, what can I get you two lovebirds to eat?"

Grateful to be back on a less dicey subject, Sam ordered a burger and fries and Dylan got the meat loaf special. Two sweet teas, which Lynne poured right away, completed their order and then they were alone again.

Dylan grinned. "There, that wasn't so bad, was it?"

"Other than lying to a perfectly nice woman I just met and then getting kicked in the shin, it was just fine." She leaned her head against the cold wood of the high-backed booth and closed her eyes. "Maybe we should just forget the whole thing." She wasn't sure she could keep the charade up for the rest of the night, let alone another few weeks.

"Hey, don't give up now. You're tougher than that."

She opened her eyes a fraction and watched him through the parted lids. "You think so?"

"I know so. The woman that held me, a potential poacher, at gunpoint in the middle of nowhere is no quitter."

He had a point. She needed to treat this like just another part of her job, another challenge to overcome. Maybe if she could compartmentalize it like that, she could make it through. "You're right. I'm not a quitter. I just wish there was another way."

"You know, if you keep saying that, you're going to hurt my feelings. Am I really that awful to be around?"

"No, not at all." In fact, if she wasn't careful she could easily get too comfortable and forget this was just for show. He was the kind of guy every woman wanted— kind, good-looking, smart and generally just fun to be around. She liked to think that when this was over they could still be friends on some level. But even that wasn't something she could count on. People moved on, relationships changed. Better to not have expectations than to end up getting hurt. "I'm just not comfortable being dishonest."

"And I respect that." He leaned toward her over the table. "If I thought you were a deceitful person, I wouldn't have agreed to help you in the first place. But really, when you think about it, is what you are doing that wrong? We aren't outright lying to people. We're just letting them think what they want to think. It's not like we're claiming to be falling in love with each other, although I suppose it could come to that. I bet a fake engagement would really seal the deal."

Sam choked, the sweet tea burning its way up her nasal passages. Love? Engagement? Dear God, what had she gotten herself into?

Dylan handed Sam an extra napkin to wipe her face, wishing he could take back his crack about the fake engagement. Obviously she was too on edge to find his lame attempt at humor anything more than horrifying. Which didn't speak well for what she thought about him, if even a *fake* engagement had her nearly choking to death in revulsion.

He mopped up the table and got them each a fresh napkin from the chrome dispenser on the table. "I'm sorry. I shouldn't have made fun of the situation, not when you're already upset about it."

"No, I'm the one who's sorry. I don't know what came over me. I guess it's easy to see why I need help with my social skills. Snorting tea probably isn't proper first-date etiquette."

"No, but technically this is our second date. Our first date was dinner at Pete's. So I think you're fine."

She shook her head, but didn't argue. Her eyes darted around the room, as if checking to see who might have witnessed her embarrassing moment, before her gaze focused in on the microphone that had been set up in the front of the restaurant.

"Have you done the trivia here before?"

"Sure, a few times. I never do very well, but it's a fun time. Lots of good-natured competition, a little teasing, that kind of thing."

"Sounds interesting. How does it work? What kinds of questions do they ask?"

"Questions can be about anything, really. Sports, history, pop culture, literature, science. As for how it works, they'll pass out scorecards in a minute. You can play as an individual or on a team—they award a prize for each category."

"Ah yes, the coveted free pie. I'm surprised fights don't break out with a prize like that." She finally seemed to be relaxing a bit.

"Who says they don't?" He winked at her. "Have you got my back if there's some kind of trivia brawl?"

"Absolutely."

"Here you go, guys, eat up quick. Trivia's going to start soon. You are going to play, right?"

"Of course. Sam and I are a team, right, Sam?"

"You know it. But I call team captain."

Lynne shook her head and patted Dylan on the shoulder. "I think you've got your hands full with this one. I like her—don't mess it up."

Sam grinned around a bite of her burger.

"You know, given that I'm the only one that's played this before, don't you think it's a bit presumptuous for you to claim the title of captain?"

She shook her head and swallowed her food. "Nope. I may not have your people skills, but a quiz game is nothing more than a glorified test. And tests I'm good at."

"Well, eat up, then, captain. You've got a reputation to uphold."

Two rounds in, he was impressed. By the final round, he was amazed. She'd gotten every question right in the topics of history, geography, science, art and literature. He'd held his own with decent if not stellar scores in sports and pop culture, but even there she'd surprised him, knowing far more recent movie titles than he did.

"You're amazing." She really was. What's more, she was finally enjoying herself. And a joyful Sam was truly something to behold. He wasn't the only one who'd noticed, either. He'd caught several men with their eye on her, and it wasn't her brain they were checking out.

"I guess being a nerd finally came in handy."

"Honey, if you're a nerd, every woman in here wishes they were, too. You've been getting jealous looks for the past hour." He picked up the menu, scanning it. "What kind of pie should we get?"

"Chocolate peanut butter. And trust me, no one is jealous of me, unless it's because of the free pie."

"No, it's because they keep catching their men staring at you, wondering who the sexy new girl is."

"Yeah, right. I think you meant smart, not sexy."

"I definitely meant sexy, although smart is part of it. Guys like a woman with brains, especially when she looks like you do. Don't sell yourself short if you don't want other people to."

She blushed and picked up the printed certificate they'd won. "Whatever. I still think they're just jealous about the pie."

"Well, let's go collect our winnings, and let them wallow in their envy." He grabbed the check that Lynne had left earlier and started for the register. When she opened her mouth as if to object, he leaned in and whispered in her ear. "Remember, it has to look like a date. No one who knows me will believe I let a woman pick up the check, so don't make a scene, okay?"

She nodded, and he was close enough to feel the breeze from her hair and smell the scent of her shampoo. Vanilla and coconuts, that's what she smelled like. Like the coconut pie that had been his favorite since he was a kid. It took all his willpower not to move closer, to see if she tasted as good as she smelled. Instead, he settled for placing a hand at the small of her back. For a second she tensed, but at his pointed look she let him steer her through the crowd.

They had to stop every few feet to accept congratulations and a bit of good-natured ribbing, as well.

"Hey, Dylan, who's the ringer?"

"Nic, hey, man!" He shook hands with his friend, and gave a quick, one-armed hug to the woman at his side. "Are you telling me your wife hasn't already told you? Because there's no way Mollie hasn't filled her in yet." The other woman reddened in acknowledgment. "Sam, this is Nic and Jillian Caruso. Jillian is best friends with Mollie, Dani's sister."

Jillian held out a hand to Sam. "Guilty as charged. Sorry, we really don't mean to be such gossips. But everything I've heard about you is nice, I promise."

Sam returned the handshake and offered one to Nic, as well. "I understand. Remember, I grew up here. Although I think I'd managed to forget about that particular aspect of small-town life while I was gone. You're the ones that bought the Sandpiper, right? I saw something about it in the newspaper when I was visiting last fall."

Jillian nodded. "About a year ago. You should come over one day and visit. I don't get out as much now that I've got little Jonathan keeping me busy, but we could have coffee and cake on the deck. I remember what it's like to be the new person in town—although I guess you're not really new. Either way, I'd love the company."

Sam agreed to visit, and Dylan could tell she was as

taken with Jillian as everyone else was. One of the kindest women he'd ever met, Jillian had come to town as a foster child and had dedicated her life to making Paradise the kind of place anyone would want to call home.

Nic glanced at his watch nervously. "All right, you ladies will have to get to know each other some other time. We've got a baby to get home to."

Jillian swatted him. "We've been gone less than two hours, and your parents are more than capable." Turning to Sam and Dylan, she continued, "It's our first time out without the baby, and he's a bit nervous."

"Johnny's only a month old! Babies are still very delicate at that age," Nic argued.

Jillian rolled her eyes. "Carusos aren't delicate. But I'm dying to see him, too, so we can go. Hope to see you guys again soon. You look great together."

Watching them leave, Dylan felt a tug of envy. Nic had found a true partner in Jillian, and she in him. Together they were more than the simple sum of their parts; they made each other better. He'd never thought much about what it would be like to have that for himself, but looking at the woman at his side, still glowing with pride from their win, he realized he might like to find out.

Sam took a deep breath of salt-tinged air as they walked outside. The temperature had cooled down since they'd gone in, and the slight chill felt good on her flushed skin. The diner had been crowded, and between the excitement of winning and the stress of meeting so many new people, she'd started to feel a bit overheated. Thankfully everyone had been nice, congratulating her on her win, with a few calling it beginner's luck and demanding a rematch next week.

"So, I'd call that a success." Dylan opened the door on his truck for her, then went around to the other side, sliding in and starting the engine.

"So it seems. I'm just glad I didn't do anything to embarrass myself or you." Other than when she'd choked on her tea, but she wasn't bringing that up if he didn't. "And Jillian and Nic seemed really nice. I mean, everyone did, but..."

"But Jillian has a way of making you feel welcome. I get it. She meant it, by the way, when she asked you to come visit her. She used to work at the local animal clinic and as much as she loves running the inn I think she's starting to get a bit restless staying home with the baby. At least that's what Mollie told me when she was at the rehab center the other day. I'm sure she'd like having the company."

Sam thought back to the names that had been mentioned earlier. "Mollie is Dani's sister, right? The photographer?"

"Right. I don't know if you noticed the photos up on the wall when you came by the office the other day, but those are her work."

"Oh, wow. They're amazing. She's really talented."

"She is. She had a show a while back at a major gallery in Atlanta, and does some work with a Florida wildlife magazine as well as freelancing."

"And she and Jillian are friends?"

"Jillian and Mollie both worked at Paradise Animal Clinic. Jillian's planning to go back part-time when the baby's a bit older. They and one of the veterinarians, Cassie Marshall, are like three peas in a pod. One can't sneeze without the other grabbing a tissue. In fact, right after Jillian got pregnant, Cassie did, too. She's due any day now. So far Mollie's held out, but I figure it's only a matter of time."

"That sounds…incredible. For them to have that kind of close friendship, I mean." She'd never had that kind of bond with anyone, other than her mother and father. And now one was gone and the other might as well be. Even if she wasn't destined to have that sort of relationship with anyone, it was nice to know it existed somewhere in the world.

"Speaking of friendships, I hope you know you've totally won over Dani. I think she likes you more than she likes me now."

Sam laughed at his hangdog expression. "I doubt it. You two seem pretty close." Just how close was something she kept wondering about. Surely Dani would have said something if there was any real history between the two of them, but still. She didn't have any right to be jealous, but she also didn't want to come between them if there was something going on.

"Close like siblings, and we fight like siblings, too. Just yesterday she spent twenty minutes telling me how lucky I am that you didn't just shoot me and put me out of my misery." He glared at her. "I never should have told her that part of the story. I'm never going to live it down."

"I don't know. Lynne at the restaurant thought it was sweet how we met."

"Lynne's a romantic."

"And you're not?" Where did that come from? She bit her lip, not sure if she even wanted to know the answer.

Instead of laughing her off, he shot her a glance of surprise, then took his time answering. "I don't know. I've never really thought about it. About romance, I mean. I was lucky enough to have parents that stayed together and are obviously still in love. And I have friends that have found that kind of relationship, people like Nic and Jillian. Maybe I've taken it for granted, that sooner or later I'll find the kind of love they have, without having to put any real thought or effort into it." He chuckled, lightening the mood. "I'm not sure if that makes me a romantic or just lazy."

"At least you believe in love and happily-ever-after."

"And you don't?"

"Not since I was a kid. Not that I don't think people ever fall in love, or at least think they do, but in my experience it's not something you can count on. People change, feelings change. All that forever stuff sounds great in a fairy tale, but in real life it just leads to hurt feelings." Why did that suddenly sound incredibly depressing?

"So I take it you're not waiting around for some knight on a white horse to show up and carry you off into the sunset?"

She snorted. "I'm pretty sure the inventory ran out on those a few centuries ago. Nowadays women save themselves—with a little help from their friends," she added. It galled her to have asked for help, but she had and she might as well acknowledge it. "Thanks for that, by the way. Helping…and being my friend."

Dylan pulled into the parking lot of her building and turned off the engine. As he had before, he came around to open her door for her, then silently walked her all the way to her front step, a tension in his movements she hadn't noticed before. Had she assumed too much by saying they were friends? Or was there something more at play?

Bracing one arm on the door above her head, he

looked right at her, his face awash in the light of a harvest moon. She absently noticed a hint of five-o'clock shadow and then shocked herself by wondering what it would feel like against her skin. This wasn't supposed to be happening, this nearly electric tension that sizzled every time he got close. And yet she found herself wondering if he was going to kiss her. She wouldn't let him, would she?

Before she could figure out what, if anything, she'd do if his lips touched hers, he leaned in and planted a soft, perfectly chaste kiss on the top of her head, sighing as he straightened. "You'd better get in before the mosquitoes find you. Sleep tight."

And then he was gone, and somehow even the moonlight seemed less bright.

Chapter Nine

Dylan sat on the split-log fence in front of the wildlife rehabilitation center, watching the sun ease closer to the horizon. Sam was picking him up in a few minutes and he was eager to see what she'd planned for their next date. Trivia night had been his idea, so she'd insisted on picking this time, and he'd been happy to oblige. Truth be told, he didn't care where they went, as long as he got to spend time with her. It had been a long three days since their last date, and even longer nights. It had taken all his strength not to kiss her for real the other evening, and he'd been restless ever since. It didn't help that she'd been by the rehab center every day to help with the morning chores. When she'd suggested volunteering, he'd had no idea what he was getting into. The more he spent time with her, the harder it was to keep his feelings in check and their relationship within the bounds she had set.

He found himself worrying about her when she was on duty and breathing a sigh of relief each morning when she showed up at the rehab center, safe and sound. His feelings were rapidly growing beyond attraction and into something much more complicated.

Adding to the confusion, he was half-convinced she was feeling the same attraction he was. More than once, he'd started to confront her about it, but pushing her like that would have betrayed the friendship she had so hesitantly accepted. He'd seen the sadness in her eyes when he'd talked about Jillian and Mollie and Cassie, and even his own friendship with Dani. Whatever curves life had thrown at her thus far, she'd handled them on her own. If he asked her for more than she was willing to give, he'd be forcing her to push him away, forcing her to be on her own again. So he'd keep his mouth shut and his hands to himself. Right now, what she needed was a friend, so that's what he would be. No matter how many cold showers he had to take.

The sound of tires on gravel carried up from the long driveway, and a minute later Sam's big truck pulled to a stop in front of him. Sliding to his feet, he brushed off his pants and walked around to the passenger side and climbed in. "So, are you going to tell me where we're going?"

She'd changed out of her uniform and looked like a cowboy's dream in tight jeans and a long-sleeved, Western-style shirt. The only thing ruining the illusion was the ball cap she wore instead of a Stetson. Seeing her this way had him wondering what she'd think of his family's ranch and the way he'd grown up. He'd sure like to see if she could ride a horse. A song lyric about saving horses and riding cowboys flashed through his mind, and he had to adjust the seat belt across his lap.

Unaware of his difficulties, Sam flashed a smug smile. "You'll figure it out when we get there."

She drove north, taking the back roads rather than heading toward the heart of Paradise, leaving him confused. There wasn't anything out this way, other than a few trailheads that led into the wilderness area. Unless… but that couldn't be right. Not for a date.

But sure enough, a few minutes later she turned off the engine and turned to him expectantly. "So, think you're up for this?"

This being the Palmetto Shooting Sports Club, Paradise Isle's only shooting range. The squat, cement block building was a big rectangle, the shooting galleries stretching toward the back and a lighted outdoor archery range off to the side. "You're taking me shooting? On a date?"

"Yup." She got out, pulling on a black backpack before circling to the rear of the truck and climbing up into the bed, where a locked metal toolbox was bolted beneath the window. When she climbed back down, she had a dull gray plastic case in one hand and a rifle slung over her shoulder. He wasn't sure if he was intimidated or turned on. Probably both. Looking over her shoulder to find him still standing in the same place, she frowned. "Is this going to be a problem?"

Great, now he felt like a wuss. "No, definitely not. It just seemed like an odd place for a date."

She shrugged. "Maybe, but a lot of hunters hang out here, and they're likely to be my best resource when it comes to tips about poachers. That's if they decide they like me. If they don't, I'm going to have problems."

He couldn't fault her logic, and he had wanted her to pick somewhere she felt comfortable. He'd just never imagined this was that place. One more facet to the jewel that was Sam. Maybe that was part of her appeal. One of the things he loved about surfing was never knowing what to expect, never knowing what the ocean might throw his way. Sam had that same way of always being herself and yet still able to surprise him. And if this was what she needed from him, he was going to give it to her. "Sounds like a plan. But you have to stop expecting people not to like you. You're a great person, and I'm sure they'll see that."

Twenty minutes later, he realized he'd had no idea what he was talking about. Busier than he would have expected on a Wednesday night, the place was full of the kind of men who took their hunting seriously. Some wore camouflage despite the indoor location; all looked like they'd crawled up out of the Florida swamps. These were the kind of men who had been hunting and living off the land for generations, and it was obvious that they didn't think much of a woman in their midst.

Sam didn't seem surprised by their attitude. He'd have said she hadn't noticed them at all if it wasn't for a certain stiffness to her movements as she signed them in. She got ammunition for both guns and hearing protection and goggles for him. "I brought my own," she explained. When he got out his wallet, she shook her head. "I've signed up for a membership online and get one guest pass a month. No charge." The attendant nodded in agreement and waved them through.

Before entering the range, they stopped to don their protective gear, then went through two sets of heavy doors. The earphones muffled the sound of gunfire, but he was thankful to find he could still hear well enough to carry on a conversation. He was about to say as much when a few of the rough-looking men he'd seen in the lobby entered.

"Look at that, the girly is gonna do some shooting. Think she's got a pink gun in that case? I hear they make those now." Laughing, the smallest of the group, a scrawny guy with a scraggly mustache, elbowed one of the other men.

"I don't think the color makes any difference when you don't hit the target," replied the one Dylan had already mentally tagged as the leader. "But maybe it helps the ladies feel pretty while they miss." He looked Sam up and down appreciatively, and Dylan felt the hair on the back of his neck prick up. He'd been in his share of fights, but he'd spent way too much time behind a desk lately. And there were three of them, counting the silent one that had walked in with the other two. He'd just have to keep his eyes open and hope Sam was smart enough to keep on ignoring them.

"You boys got something you want to say?" Sam's taunt echoed, and Dylan's gut clenched.

So much for ignoring them.

Sam could feel the tension radiating off Dylan, but there was no way she was going to let herself be insulted or intimidated by anyone. Right now, they didn't know who she was, and honestly probably didn't mean any harm. She'd grown up around men like this, and nine times out of ten they were more bark than bite. In her experience, the real backwoods boys were a lot more trustworthy than some of the city folks she knew, but sometimes needed a little reminding when it came to manners.

"We're just wondering what a pretty thing like you is doing in place like this." That from the smaller one, who seemed to be the instigator.

"Hey, if the lady wants to shoot, let her shoot." The bigger one smiled, as if doing her a favor. "She probably needs all the practice she can get, right, boys?"

They nodded, and she smiled. This was going to be too easy.

"You know, you're probably right. In fact, maybe one of you could show me how it's done?"

Dylan started to object, but she waved him off. She'd baited the trap; now she needed them to walk into it.

"Sure thing, honey." The big one again. "I've taught these guys all they know. I'd be happy to do a little one-on-one with you. The name's Beau."

Dylan took another step closer, but to his credit he stayed quiet and let her do the talking.

"Well, Beau it's nice to meet you. I'm Sam…Samantha." If they were going to play the girl card, she'd use it to her advantage. "What do you think, rifles or hand-guns first?"

"Rifles. Long guns have a kick, but they're a bit easier to aim for beginners."

"Whatever you say." Trying to sound nonchalant, she ignored his patronizing tone. She'd heard far worse from the other recruits at the academy. Words weren't important here; actions were. She watched as the burly man loaded his rifle and then clipped a paper bull's-eye to a cable overhead, sending it downrange. She held her breath in anticipation as he sighted and then fired.

Reeling the target back, he was pointing to the holes

scattered across the target. "See how all of them are in the colored circles? It's best if you can cluster them, like these three are, but as long as they all hit on the target you're doing pretty well."

She nodded in real appreciation. He wasn't a bad shot, not at all. She'd seen experienced hunters sometimes miss the mark entirely, especially when they were trying to impress someone.

"All right, sugar, go ahead and give it a try."

Already loading her weapon, a Winchester that had been her grandfather's, she barely heard him. When she handled a loaded gun, her concentration was all turned inward, on to the power that she held in her hands.

Dylan had already sent her target out, silently supporting her. She took a few slow breaths, trying to slow her heart rate. Then, with her sights locked on the target, she squeezed the trigger. Using the lever action to chamber another round, she repeated the process five more times. Each time a bullet ripped through the paper, and when Dylan pulled the target in she knew without looking that she'd nailed it.

"Hot damn! Let me see that!" Beau grabbed the paper and traced his finger over the single hole in the bull's-eye. All five bullets had pierced the paper in the same spot.

Turning to her, respect in his eyes, he let out a long whistle. "Lady, where did you learn to shoot like that?"

"Well, my father taught me the basics. The rest I picked up at the academy."

"Whoa, you're a cop?" The men behind him looked nervously at each other at the revelation.

"I'm Officer Sam Finley with the Florida Fish and Wildlife Commission."

The man sheepishly held out a hand, regret clear as

day on his face. "Well, Officer, it's nice to meet you. I hope you know we didn't mean any offense."

She shook his hand and smiled. "None taken. And you can call me Sam."

"Well, Sam, you're the best shot I've seen in a long time. Reminds me of...wait, did you say Finley? Are you Tom Finley's daughter?"

"Yes, sir. I told you my daddy taught me to shoot."

"Well, that does explain it. He could shoot the wings off a mosquito. Haven't seen him around here in ages, though. If you see him, tell him Beau Griggson says hey."

A small worm of sadness twisted through her gut, but she kept her smile bright. "Yeah, he keeps to himself most of the time. But I'll make sure to tell him if I see him." Turning back to Dylan, she took a second to catch her breath. Now that the adrenaline was wearing off, her nerves were trying to take over. Funny how challenging them had been easier than just talking with them. Hopefully she'd manage the conversation part as well as the shooting. "Beau, let me introduce you to my friend Dylan. He runs the Wildlife Rehab Center over on the other side of the preserve."

Dylan offered his right hand, his left resting possessively on the small of her back. "Good to meet you."

"Yeah, well, could have been better. I've heard good things about that rehab center. My little girl found an injured bird a while back and my wife and her brought it to your place. She was really upset over that bird, but you all fixed it up and got it back flying again."

"They do amazing things over there," Sam interjected, sensing an opportunity. "I took over a fawn the other day. Poachers got its mother, shot it from their truck, it looks like. Don't suppose you guys have heard anything about that?"

"No, ma'am." Behind him, the other two shook their heads in agreement. "We don't take kindly to poachers. There's no sportsmanship in it."

"That's the truth." She pulled a card from her backpack and handed one to each of the men. "If you do hear anything, give me a call."

"Will do. And you tell your daddy we'd love to see him out here some time."

"I will." Not that it would do any good. She'd made some progress today on the job front, but dealing with her father was going to be a lot more difficult.

Dylan waited until the group of hunters had moved out of earshot before confronting Sam. "That was amazing. No—you were amazing. You had that planned all along, didn't you?"

She shrugged, but her smile gave her away. "Maybe. I knew I could outshoot them."

"Obviously." He still couldn't get over what a marksman she was. Or was it markswoman? "But how did you know he'd be impressed, rather than just angry or defensive?"

"I didn't. I just had a hunch."

"A hunch. You took on three large, armed men based on a hunch? You are one brave woman, Sam Finley. Remind me not to make you angry."

She rolled her eyes. "It's a shooting range, and everyone is armed. Besides, they just look scary. Men like that have their own code of honor. Rough around the edges, yes. But not dangerous, usually."

Usually, she said. Most of the time he forced himself

to forget the kind of danger her job entailed, but events like this made him face it head-on. He hated knowing she put herself at risk, and hated even more that there was nothing he could do about it, other than hope and pray that she could take care of herself. Tonight that had been enough. Heaven help the day it wasn't. "Well, I'm glad you were right. And it seems like you won them over. Think they'll call if they come across any information?"

"I'd like to say yes, but it's hard to know for sure. As much as my shooting impressed them, I'm still new. They'll be waiting to see how I conduct myself, to see if I'm trustworthy. But it was a good first step."

"So, what now?"

"Now it's your turn. Have you ever shot before?"

"A bit. I had a BB gun, like any ranch kid, and my father made sure we could all use the shotgun if we needed to. But it's been a long time. I'm certainly nowhere near your caliber."

"Not many people are." She winked. "Ever shot a handgun?"

"No, but I'm willing to learn, since I've got Annie Oakley for a teacher."

She stuck her tongue out at him, and pulled another ball cap out of her backpack. Sticking it on his head, she pulled it down snugly. "To keep the hot shells from getting caught in your hair. I'll go first, talking you through it, and then you can try."

Dylan watched Sam's deft hands load rounds into a plastic magazine. "This is a Glock 21. It's 45 caliber, so it has a strong kick, but all the stopping power you could need." Slamming the full clip into the butt of the gun, she showed him how to rack the slide and chamber a round. "Most people do it this way." She demonstrated, holding the gun in one hand, pointed downrange, and pulling back on the top with the other. "As a man you've got the hand strength to do that. A lot of women, or people with arthritis or other issues with hand strength, will do it like this, to transfer the load to the biceps." She demonstrated again, this time holding it in front of her and pushing with both hands, at opposite angles. "Pushing muscles are stronger than pulling muscles. Most of the time it won't matter for someone your size, but if you're ever injured, it's good to know both."

Turning the barrel downrange, she continued her narration. "Never point a gun anywhere you aren't willing to shoot. That includes an unloaded weapon."

"All guns are loaded guns. I remember."

"Sorry, I forgot you grew up around them. Not everyone does, and too many people treat them like a toy."

"It's fine, better safe than sorry."

She nodded in agreement. "Okay, so the next rule is never put your finger on the trigger until you're ready to shoot. Just rest it here, alongside, until you're committed."

He nodded that he understood.

"Okay, now for stance, you have a few options, but the steadiest is going to be a Modified Weaver stance. Legs shoulder distance apart, with the leg on the shooting side a bit behind the other, and your weight forward over the toes to absorb the recoil. Arms are extended and locked. Head should be level. Bring the sights up, line up your target and squeeze the trigger smoothly."

Her shot echoed through the building.

"The next bullet will chamber automatically. Just continue to fire until you're empty." Nine more shots rang out in quick succession, clustering just to the right of center.

"Okay, now I definitely don't want to make you angry." Moreover, he was starting to feel like a fish out of water, desperately out of his element. He was a modern guy—he didn't need to be better than a woman at everything—but he also didn't want to make a fool of himself in front of her. When he was interested in a woman he liked to impress her. And despite all the reasons he shouldn't be, he was definitely interested in Sam.

Taking the empty magazine she'd discharged, he tried to remember the movements she'd used. Pushing the bullets in took more strength than he would have thought, but the magazine slid into the gun easily once it was full.

"Okay, now rack the slide…good."

He kept the gun pointed downrange and settled into the stance Sam had shown him, making sure to stagger his feet. Getting knocked on his butt would definitely end any chance of looking good. Taking aim, he said a little prayer that he'd at least hit the target, and squeezed the trigger.

"Awesome!" Sam bounced on her toes in his peripheral vision. Encouraged, he reset his stance and tried again, repeating her instructions in his head with each squeeze of the trigger. When the last round had fired, he set the gun down carefully and let out the breath he'd been holding.

Sam pushed the button to pull back the target and let out a whoop. All but one bullet had hit the target, and about half were within the inner three rings. "Not bad, surfer boy, not bad at all."

"Thanks, but I know when I'm outclassed."

"Maybe, but you handled it well. A lot of guys get bent

out of shape when a woman is better at something than they are. But you were willing to go along with what I wanted, even knowing I had more experience than you. And on top of that, you let me handle those guys, instead of getting all macho and taking over. So, thank you, it means a lot to me."

"If the men you've been around are scared off by a strong woman, you need to hang out with a better class of man."

She cocked her head and looked up at him, as if trying to gauge his sincerity. "Maybe I do, at that."

Something in her tone told him she meant it, that she was feeling some of the same attraction and intensity he was. But before he could find a way to ask his phone buzzed in his pocket. Checking the screen, he bit back a curse. "It's one of the night shift volunteers. She needs me back right away—she says it's an emergency."

Chapter Ten

Dylan made good time to the clinic, pushing the speed limit on the back roads. The message had been cryptic, and no one had responded when he had texted back asking for more information. He'd also tried calling the back line at the center with no success. Trish's text hadn't given much information, leaving him to his own imagination. None of the animals had been critical, but it was possible one could have taken a turn for the worse. Or maybe it wasn't an animal, but something structural, like another leak. Except it hadn't rained in days. The most likely scenario was that someone had shown up after hours with an injured creature, but the protocol in that situation was to page the vet, not him.

By the time they pulled into the parking lot, he had enough adrenaline pumping through his veins to jump-start a jet engine. He was out of the truck before Sam had a chance to put it in Park, but by the time he was turning his key in the front door she had caught up. Part of his brain processed that she had her duty weapon holstered on her hip, instead of in the case she'd used earlier. Surely she didn't expect to need it? Of course, since he had no idea what was going on, he didn't argue against it.

His key turned easily, and he pushed open the door, blinking against the bright overhead lights. Sitting in his chair, her feet on his desk, was not Trish, the volunteer who had texted him, but Dani.

"You got here quick." She stood and walked over, giving Sam a hug. "And I didn't know you were with him. That's a bonus, so now it will be two against one."

"What are you talking about? What's the emergency?"

The sound of nails clicking on the hard floor drew his attention. "Did one of the animals get out?"

"It's more that one got in," Dani hedged. Before he could question her further, a small, gray-muzzled beagle made his way from between the desks to stand at Dani's feet. "Meet Toby."

Dylan's eyelid started to twitch. "Dani, we're a wildlife refuge, not the pound. We don't take in homeless dogs. And how on earth did you get in here, anyway?"

"Trish let me in. I told her there was an emergency with Toby here, and asked her to text you."

"Why couldn't you text me yourself?"

She looked away. "Um, my phone battery was dead."

Bull. She knew he'd have just called her and asked for more information if she'd been the one to contact him. He'd have a word with Trish tomorrow, but in all reality the poor teenager hadn't stood a chance against Dani. "And Trish is where now?"

"She left a few minutes ago. She was done with the night chores, and I told her I'd be fine here by myself."

And the young volunteer had probably jumped at the chance to avoid being part of this particular confrontation. "But that's not important. What matters is poor Toby here. He belonged to the grandmother of one of my clients, but she died and there's no one to take him in."

"Aw, the poor thing." Sam knelt down and stroked the dog's head. "That's terrible. Can't your client's family keep him?"

"No, the youngest boy has asthma and is allergic to dogs. And there's no one else. I'd take him myself, but my apartment doesn't allow dogs."

Sam sighed. "Mine has a one-pet maximum, and I've already got Cheesy."

"Okay, I get that he's running out of options, but like I said, we're not equipped to handle pet boarding. Maybe Cassie could help? She's taken in foster dogs before."

"You mean nine-months-pregnant-due-any-day Cassie? I'm sure she would help, if I asked her, but I'm not going to add one more thing to that woman's plate right now. And before you ask, Mollie is in Atlanta, and even if she wasn't, this dog has lived in one place his whole life. Getting used to one new home is going to be hard enough. It's not fair to ask him to try to transition to traveling between two places."

She had a point. Mollie and her husband, Noah, traveled back and forth between Atlanta and Paradise, splitting their time between the island they loved and the more metropolitan area. Mollie's dog managed, but he was younger and not dealing with the loss of the only owner he'd ever known. "What about Jillian?" he asked, although he was pretty sure he already knew the answer.

Sam looked up from where she was snuggling the little dog. "Isn't Jillian the one that just had a baby?"

"Yes," Dani answered, glaring at him. "We can't ask a woman with a one-month-old to take on a new—well, an old—dog." Turning to Sam, she smiled. "I knew you'd be on my side."

"What side? Do you seriously expect me to keep him here? I couldn't if I wanted to. We're full to the gills." But even as he protested he started mentally rearranging patients, trying to see where he could fit a dog in among the possums and pelicans.

"No, of course not," Dani assured him, grinning. "You're going to adopt him."

"No, I'm not. You can't just trick me into coming here with some false emergency, then inform me I've adopted a dog." Even in Paradise, things didn't work that way.

"You've said a million times that you want to get a dog. And this one needs a home."

"I meant a puppy, not a senior citizen. And something big, like a golden retriever that I could take jogging on the beach. Toby's going to have to find another sucker."

"So you're just going to turn him away?" He tried to ignore the disappointment in Sam's voice, but it was no good. He had two options here—one choice would have him looking like a hero in her eyes, the other like a cad.

Sinking down into a crouch, he called the dog over. "Hey, Toby, what do you think? Do you want to come live with me?"

A quick thump of the tail and a wet dog kiss sealed the deal. He was going home heavy one geriatric beagle.

Sam watched Dylan drive off with Toby hanging his head out of the back window before climbing up into the cab of her own truck.

"Thanks for your help in there. He never stood a chance." Dani looked up at her with a grin.

"Thanks, but I really don't think I did anything."

"Are you kidding? One look from you and he was ready to agree to anything. That man's got it bad. I almost feel sorry for taking advantage of the situation. Not quite, but almost."

Sam replayed Dani's words in her head. "What situation? Just because we're…dating? It's not like it's serious. We barely know each other."

"Trust me, it's serious. At least for him. My career depends on me knowing how to read people, knowing what they're thinking even when they're saying the exact opposite. And that man is falling fast and hard for you."

Before Sam could string together a coherent argument, Dani was gone, waving as she climbed into her little convertible. Left standing there, she tried to rationalize Dani's words. After all, she didn't know that the relationship between Sam and Dylan was all for show, so of course she'd think there were romantic feelings involved.

On the other hand, Dani and Dylan were good friends. Maybe she was picking up on something that Sam hadn't. Yes, she knew he had been attracted to her, enough to ask her out, and she'd started to feel like they were forging a friendship, but could it be more than that? Surely he wasn't really falling for her. Not now.

Checking the directions he'd given her, she steered down a narrow canopy road. She'd planned to allow him and his new pet to bond, but as she was leaving he'd suggested they order a pizza to share while he got the dog settled in to his new home, to make up for cutting the date short. It had seemed a reasonable plan before, but after Dani's comments she wasn't so sure. It was too late to cancel, though; he would have already ordered the food and would be expecting her.

Turning onto his street, she slowed to check the house numbers. Most of the homes were older, on large, tree-covered lots. Halfway down she spotted Dylan's pickup and pulled in behind him. His house was one of the smaller ones on the street, an older cabin style with a wooded yard that backed right up to the wilderness area. He could walk out his back door and hike for miles if he wanted. She thought of her own concrete apartment block with a stab of jealousy.

Her knock was met with an enthusiastic braying, and she stifled a grin. It seemed Toby was already settling in to the role of watchdog. Dylan opened the door and glared at her. "I blame you for this."

"For him being loud? I think that's just what beagles do."

"Yeah, well, if you and Dani hadn't ganged up on me, he'd be doing it somewhere else." His words were harsh, but he was scratching the dog's head as he said them. And glancing around she could see he'd set up a folded blanket for a bed and filled the food and water bowls he'd borrowed from the rehab center. He might talk a tough game, but he was a big softy at heart.

"I think he ended up right where he belongs. Didn't you, boy?" Toby wagged his tail, but stayed at Dylan's side, leaning against his leg. "He certainly seems to have bonded quickly with you."

"That's the kibble talking. I'm pretty sure he'd do anything for food. Speaking of which, don't leave your pizza plate where he can get it. He already tried to swipe a piece, and I don't want to be cleaning beagle puke at midnight."

"I'll keep that in mind." She followed him to the kitchen, where a small, high-top table by the window held a pizza box and paper plates. "Nice place, by the way."

"Thanks. It needs a lot of work still, but I like it."

She chewed a bite of pizza and let her eyes roam. The eat-in kitchen was small, with old-fashioned but clean Formica counters and what looked to be brand-new stainless-steel appliances. Modern meets retro seemed to be the theme, and it carried over into the living area, where a flat-screened television hung on 1960-style wood-paneled walls.

Noticing the direction of her gaze, he shrugged. "Like I said, it needs work."

"Maybe some updating," she agreed. "But the location makes up for it." She finished her pizza and shifted over to the couch. Toby immediately jumped up with her, curling up into her lap with a contented sigh. Sam raised an eyebrow at Dylan. "Is he okay to be up here?"

"It doesn't look like I have much of a say in the matter."

"Probably not." But she was glad he was being so kind to the old dog. Stroking his fur, she closed her eyes. It had been such a long day, she'd earned a few minutes of rest. When the couch shifted, she looked up to find Dylan had joined her, his body only inches from hers.

Dani's words echoed in her head. If he was developing feelings for her, she should try to squash them. She certainly shouldn't sit snuggled on the couch with him, and yet she couldn't bring herself to move away. Not even when he reached to pet the dog, shifting even closer. His thigh pressed against hers, warming her body. They sat like that for several long minutes, the sound of a light rain on the roof and the feel of the soft fur of the dog in her lap relaxing her so much she found it hard to keep her eyes open. When she started to nod, Dylan reached his arm around her, pulling her closer to rest her head on his shoulder. Warning bells rang, but this time she ignored them.

"This is nice." Dylan's voice rumbled softly through her, sending up a tingling awareness.

"It is, but it isn't real. It doesn't mean anything." Even as she said it, she snuggled closer, seeking the solid strength of him.

"It could." His hand stroked her hair, but he held the rest of him still. It was as if he wanted her to know that if anything happened, it would be on her to make the first move. All she had to do was turn her head the slightest bit, and his lips would be right there. Kissing him would be as easy as breathing, but a huge mistake.

"No, it can't. Not yet, anyway." How could she explain to him what she was just starting to understand herself? "I need to get my life in order before I can even think about adding anything else." She could stop there, but for once she wanted to put into words the fears that haunted her at night. Maybe if she said them out loud, here with him, where she was safe, they'd let her sleep tonight. "Dylan, I'm scared." His hand stilled in her hair. "No, I'm terrified. I've worked my whole life with one goal, and if I don't get things right, that could be taken away from me. I'm scared of losing my job, of never fitting in in the one place I think of as home. I just can't risk anything else right now. I'm sorry."

She should get up now and go home to her apartment. Instead, she twined her fingers though his, trying to let him know that she wasn't ready to move forward, but for now at least she wasn't going to run away.

* * *

Sam had stayed way too long at Dylan's, dozing on the couch until well after midnight. But Toby's snores had finally roused her, and she'd slipped out without waking the dog or his master. Now she was in her own bed, alone and wide awake. She'd never thought of herself as a lonely person, but tonight she found herself missing the quiet company she'd found at Dylan's. Nights like this, when sleep wouldn't come and the silence was nearly deafening, were when she missed her mother the most.

Some of her favorite memories were of sitting at the kitchen table with her mom, sharing cookies and milk in the wee hours of the morning—her mother's remedy for nightmares. Better than the sweets had been having her mother's undivided attention. She'd been an amazing listener, never judging, always taking whatever childhood fear Dani had so seriously.

What would you say now, Mom, if you were here?

Her mother would have approved of Dylan: of that she was certain. Like him, she'd been the kind of person everyone was comfortable with, who made friends without even trying. Samantha had taken after her father, being more reserved. They'd basked in the reflected light of her mother, happy because she was happy, listening to her retell the latest tales she'd picked up while shopping or visiting.

Without her mom there, her father had withered away, unable to find another center to his life. Sam had pushed on, but how much had been just going through the motions? Here she was, a grown woman still scared to face the same old fears. She liked to think she had made some progress, that her mother would be proud of how hard she'd worked. But her mom, more than most, had known life wasn't about work or career accolades. It was about family and friends, and those were the areas Sam couldn't seem to make headway in.

At first, she'd accepted her father's distance. They'd both been grieving and he'd had the added stress of taking care of an adolescent girl. She had done her best to be unobtrusive, staying at the library after school or staying in her room, out of his hair. But he'd sent her away anyway, and with each passing year the rift between them had grown deeper. No perfect report card, no scholarship, had been enough to bring back the father she'd once known, the one who put her pictures on the fridge and bragged about his "smart cookie."

She'd hoped this job might be the one thing that could help them find common ground, but so far even that hadn't worked. He hadn't wanted her to be a wildlife officer, and no matter how well she did in the academy he'd refused to change his mind. Even finishing top in her class hadn't won him over.

And maybe it was time to stop trying. She *was* making progress with the people of Paradise, maybe she needed to focus on that. If her father came around that would be great, but she was tired of swimming against the current, and if she was going to keep her head above water something needed to change. She needed to change.

She wasn't going to give up, she didn't know how. But maybe she could fight for herself for a change, instead of fighting for his approval. She'd been living for her father, and maybe even for the ghost of her mother, for so long it was hard to imagine anything else. But being in Paradise made her want more. She'd come here hoping to force some connections in order to succeed at her job, but now that wasn't enough. Yes, she wanted to be a good wildlife officer, but now, instead of just wanting a means to an end, contacts in the community, people to help her with her job, she wanted friendship, the kind that Dani and Dylan had, the kind that Jillian and her friends had. The kind of friends her mother had once had, so long ago.

Maybe if she took some time to focus on those things, she wouldn't need her father's approval.

Of course, there was one other thing she wanted, something she almost didn't dare to think of. But she could dream, and as she finally felt her eyes drift closed it was Dylan she was dreaming of.

Chapter Eleven

Dylan dumped the last feed bucket of the morning into the stainless-steel bowl Sam had just washed out. "Chow time, Harry. Come and get it."

Harry the gopher tortoise blinked once before starting his slow, scratching crawl to his breakfast of greens and chopped vegetables. Before Harry they'd fed a baby alligator, a panther, three skunks, a pelican and an armadillo. His other Saturday volunteer had handled the raccoons, bobcats and an owl.

"He's the last one, right?" Sam coiled the hose as she spoke, looking as gorgeous as ever in a pair of faded jeans and a football jersey.

"Yeah, we're done." Which meant she'd be leaving, and he didn't want to say goodbye. Not yet. They'd made tentative plans for dinner at a local restaurant, but that was hours away. He didn't want to wait, and he didn't want to put on a show. He wanted something real. "So, got any big plans for the rest of the day?"

She shrugged. "Not really. I may have to break down and hit the grocery store. I'm at that point where I'm so sick of takeout and frozen dinners that I might be willing to risk my own cooking."

"I guess that means you aren't secretly a gourmet cook."

She laughed. "Hardly. I can burn water with the worst of them. Another trait I inherited from my father, I'm afraid. But sometimes I just crave a real, home-cooked meal and so I convince myself this time will be different."

An idea struck him. "What if I could provide you with a home-cooked meal that will leave you begging for more?"

"Are you offering to cook?"

"No. I mean, I could make us something, but what I have in mind is way better."

"I told you, I'm not in the mood for takeout or a restaurant."

"Not what I'm suggesting."

She stopped, and he could tell he had her interest. "Okay, I'll bite. What do you have in mind?"

"Dinner at my family's ranch. They always do a big early supper on Saturdays, with an open invitation for family and friends. It's a beautiful day for a drive, and you can't beat the food. Everything's from scratch."

She wiped her hands on her jeans. "Thanks, but I'll pass. I'm not exactly dressed for a big family dinner."

"You look fantastic. Besides, it's a working ranch, not a country club. Everyone comes as they are. You'll fit right in, I promise."

She leaned against the building, the sun catching the

strands of gold that ran through her dark hair. Shoulders slumping, she looked tired and overworked. No wonder— given the long, physical hours she was putting in at her job, plus volunteering daily at the rehab center. Add in the strain of the charade they were keeping up and he wasn't quite sure how she was still standing. She needed a break from everything, and he wanted to give that to her.

Shading her eyes, she looked up at him. "I don't know. It seems a lot of trouble and time without much payoff. I mean, yes, it would be good to have them on my side, but it's your family. Couldn't you just call and put in a good word for me? Or do you think they need to see us together to buy it?"

He bit his tongue, wanting to tell her to just forget about the stupid agreement, but that wouldn't accomplish anything. "Sam, this isn't about trying to convince them of anything. They don't need to think we're dating to be on your side. They'll respect you by virtue of your badge, and if they ever need to report anything they'll call. You don't have to win them over."

"Then why invite me?"

"Because I think it would be fun."

She just stared, so he tried again. "I'd like to spend the day with you. And I'd like to show you where I grew up. I think you'll like it out there." He stuck his hands in his pockets and looked her in the eye. "As your friend, I'm asking you to have dinner with me and my family. That's all."

Sam's eyes went wide. Good, maybe that meant she was finally getting it. He wasn't hanging out with her just because of some stupid agreement. He wanted to spend time with her—actually, he wanted a lot more than that—but some downtime, without the pressure of trying to impress anyone or act a part, would be a good place to start.

"Just dinner?"

"Just dinner." He'd keep his hands in his pockets the whole darned day if he had to. He wasn't going to push her, not when they were making some progress.

"What will you tell your parents about me?"

"I've already told them about you. We talk on the phone pretty often."

She tensed, crossing her arms against her body. "And what did you say? Did you tell them about our agreement?"

"I did. They don't care about that, although my mom did say it was a shame that you were under such pressure. And that people would come around in their own time."

"So they weren't shocked? Or offended that I'd roped you into something dishonest?"

He laughed, startling a nearby squirrel, who chattered angrily before returning to his meal of acorns. "Honey, no one thinks you've besmirched my honor, I assure you. If anything, they think I'm taking advantage of you."

"But how? What are you getting out of it?"

"The company of a beautiful woman, of course." She rolled her eyes. "I'm pretty sure they think this was all my idea, a way to trap you into spending time with me."

"And you're sure they won't mind me just showing up?"

"Trust me, they'll love you." Because Sam, whether she knew it or not, was way too easy to love.

Sam sat nervously in the passenger seat of Dylan's pickup as they headed out of town. Straight ahead was the arch of the bridge connecting Paradise Isle to the mainland. Out the window on either side stretched the Intracoastal Waterway, a rich ecosystem that served as a breeding ground for fish and birds, as well as a favorite recreational area for the people of Palmetto County. Today there were nearly a dozen boats dotting the calm waters, mostly small fishing vessels, but she spotted one of the Fish and Wildlife patrol, as well. Sam had ended up working the forests and other land areas, but some officers were assigned to the waterways, making sure people followed the law regarding the size and number of fish they could catch. Numerous species had been overfished in these waters but were now making a comeback, thanks to tighter regulations and the hard work of the men and women who enforced them.

Once on the other side of the bridge, the scenery changed from the bright blue of the waterway to the green of the freshwater marshes that dotted this part of the coast. Blue herons, egrets and spoonbills called this area home, and she always tried to keep an eye out for them. Some people loved the mountains or the desert, but when it came to beauty Sam preferred the ever changing landscape of the Florida coast.

Where else could you go from the beach to marsh to grasslands in the span of just a few minutes? And she knew that in a few more miles it would change again, becoming drier, with clumps of oak and stands of pine forest, the perfect environment for white-tailed deer and wild turkey. She patrolled this area often, and the beauty and variety never failed to impress her. Something about the timelessness of it soothed her soul, smoothing down the sharp edges left from day-to-day life.

Leaning her head on the window, she found herself lulled by the motion of the car and serenity of the scenery into a half sleep, dozing until she felt their speed slow. Opening her eyes, she saw that they'd just turned off the highway onto a two-lane road snaking through the woods. About a mile later the paved road turned to gravel and the trees opened up, revealing open pastures dotted with cattle. "Is this your land?"

"My family's, yes. The house is up around the next bend."

A minute later they turned east and drove under an arching sign that read Paradise Ranch.

"They named it after the island?"

"Yes and no. My grandfather did live on the island for a few years before buying the ranch, but it's more that he considered this part of Florida to be his version of paradise, heaven on earth. It makes for some interesting postal mishaps, but I can't argue with his premise."

Certainly not. The place was gorgeous, in that rugged old-Florida way. The house itself was a traditional, two-story structure, with a wraparound veranda that was screened to protect against Florida's legendary mosquitoes. Several outbuildings were scattered across the surrounding grounds, as well as a large vegetable garden and what looked like a fire pit.

Dylan drove slowly past the house and parked in the shade of a steel barn next to two other trucks and a fat-tired all-terrain vehicle. He'd barely shut off the engine when a pair of Australian shepherds came running out from the barn. Dylan laughed as they jumped into the bed of the truck, barking and scratching at the rear window. "Jett, Zip, knock it off. You'll scare the pretty lady."

"No, they won't." She climbed out of the cab and walked around to the back of the truck. "You guys are quite the welcoming committee, aren't you?" The dogs nearly fell over themselves trying to sniff and lick her, and from the cab she heard Toby whine in jealousy.

"She still loves you, too, you old fool." Dylan helped the older, small dog down and then stood over him ready to intervene as the two farm shepherds jumped down and investigated the newcomer.

"Who are you calling an old fool?" The gravelly voice came from the shadows inside the barn, where the afternoon sun couldn't quite penetrate. A moment later, a lean, older man stepped out and embraced Dylan.

"Not you, Dad. You never age. I was talking to this old guy." He pointed to Toby, who was now happily rolling in the dirt with the other dogs.

"And where did he come from?"

Dylan sighed. "It's a long story. Let's say I'm a sucker and leave it at that."

The older man laughed and slapped him on the back. "You always were. But I'm glad to see you. It's been too long." He turned to Sam, and offered a weathered hand. "Now then, you must be that wildlife officer Dylan was telling us about. I have to say, you're just as pretty as he said you were."

Sam felt her cheeks heat. Dylan had told his father she was pretty? Flustered, she took his hand and nearly forgot to say something in return. "Thanks…it's nice to meet you, Mr. Turner."

"You can call me Ken. And the pleasure is all mine." He raked Dylan over with his gaze. "Does your mama know you're here?"

"Not yet, we just pulled in a minute ago."

"Well, you go tell her hello, and then when you get a minute maybe you could take a look at the books with me." He winked at Sam. "Might as well get some use out of all those fancy degrees."

"Come one, Sam, let's go introduce you to the rest of

the family." Dylan placed a hand on her back, guiding her toward the house. "Dad, I'll find you once we make the rounds."

Sam kept pace with Dylan's long strides. "Your father seems nice."

"He's a good guy. Tough but fair, and so smart it's scary."

"So you two are close, even though you didn't stay on the ranch like your siblings?" She knew all too well what it felt like to go against a parent's wishes, but she didn't sense that kind of rift between Dylan and his father.

"Honestly, I sometimes think they're glad I didn't stay. Miranda and Seth do a great job, but they can fight like cats and dogs. Add me to the mix and things sometimes got a bit crazy. This way, I can pop in for a visit, then leave before we all get on each other's nerves."

"That makes sense." Sibling rivalry was something she'd read about, but as an only child never experienced for herself.

They went up the wide, wooden steps to a screen door that opened onto the shaded patio area. Her first impression was one of comfort. The low eaves kept the hot Florida sun at bay, and paddle fans overhead provided a steady breeze. On this side of the house there were two rocking chairs as well as a cushioned bench swing. Passing them, Dylan led her around the corner to the back of the house, where an oversize picnic table and full outdoor kitchen area dominated the space.

Dylan slowed in front of a set of open French doors, motioning Sam to be quiet. Treading silently, he slipped into the house, where a tall, dark-haired woman was working at the counter with her back to the door. With a grin on his face, Dylan swooped her into a hug, startling a scream out of her.

"Dylan!" She swatted at him, laughing and trying to appear stern at the same time. "One of these days, you are going to scare me to death doing that. Now put me down."

"Yes, ma'am." He motioned Sam to come in, and turned back to his mother. "Sam, this is my mom, Adele Turner. Mom, this is Sam, the one I told you about. She's been craving a home-cooked meal—"

"So instead of taking the time to make her one yourself you dragged her all the way out here." She smiled at Sam, the fine lines around her eyes crinkling with mirth. "I swear, I did teach him to cook. I taught all of them, fat lot of good it did me."

"We just know there's no sense in trying to compete with the master."

"Flattery won't get you dinner, but helping might. You can make the salad while I finish this cake."

"Sorry, but I already promised Dad I'd take a look at the books with him."

She sighed. "Fine. But don't even try to get out of helping with the dishes later."

"I can make the salad," Sam offered. "I'm barging in on your family meal—the least I can do is chop a few vegetables."

Adele smiled at Sam, then jabbed Dylan in the belly with a wooden spoon. "You see, that's what appreciation looks like. Now go, so Sam and I can talk about you behind your back."

Dylan didn't like the sound of that, but he also knew better than to argue with his mother. His dad might look fiercer, but in comparison he was a pushover.

He found his father in the study, sitting at the same desk Dylan's grandfather had used once upon a time. Photos of the family lined the walls, everything from holiday photos to candids taken at the county fair. Dylan's favorite, though, was one of his parents taken after they'd spent the day repairing hurricane damage to the barn. Both were dirty and tired, but the love between them shone through the mud and sweat. They were true partners, able to face anything as long as they had each other.

Noticing his gaze, his father nodded in approval. "A good woman makes everything better. Even hurricanes. Of course, sometimes love is the refuge, sometimes it's the storm. You have to ride it out to know which way it will end."

Ignoring his father's attempt at advice, Dylan moved behind the desk and took a glance at the spreadsheet showing on the computer. "Anything in particular you're worried about?"

His father tapped his fingers nervously on the edge of the desk, his lips pursed in thought. Dylan's heart squeezed. Dad didn't get nervous, not over things like money. A sick calf or the degradation of the Floridan aquifer, maybe. But money was just a means to an end for him. Pulling a chair around from the other side of the desk, Dylan sat and took a harder look at the numbers. Everything looked in order, but something had his normally steadfast father worried. "Everything looks okay. You should end the year in the black, with a decent profit."

"Good, that's what I thought, too. But I'm more concerned about the bigger picture. I thought maybe you could take a look at the investments—I've got a statement here somewhere—and maybe the insurance policies, too. Basically, I want to know if everything's in order to keep this ranch going for the long term, or if I need to be making any changes."

"Sure, I can do that. But is there something going on I should know about? Is everything okay around here?"

"Everything's fine. I'm just not getting any younger, and I want to make sure things are taken care of after I'm gone. I don't want to leave any financial burdens for your mother or you kids."

Dylan stilled, his hand hovering over the computer mouse. The idea of his father being gone, dying, was incomprehensible. He was the bedrock their family was built on. If something was wrong with him...just the thought was enough to have bile rising in his throat. "Are you sick? Does Mom know?"

"No, I'm not sick, son. Just old. None of us lives forever, and I've reached a point where I want to be sure things are taken care of, that's all."

The temporary panic he'd felt retreated a bit, leaving a bad taste in his mouth and a lump in his throat. Dylan had always known his father was older than most of his friends' parents, but until now it hadn't seemed important. The nearly fifteen-year difference in his parents' ages hadn't seemed important, either, but there were more lines on his father's face than he remembered, where his mother still looked to be in the prime of her life. "All right, I'll take a look." It still seemed early, but if it would make his father happy there wasn't any harm in making sure everything was taken care of. "In fact, I'll print out some of this, if that's okay, and go over it later when I can take my time."

A knowing smile lit up his father's face. "You just want to hurry back to that pretty young lady of yours."

"Is it that obvious?"

"That you're in love with her? Probably not to every-one, but you look at her the way I look at your mother. Like she's a gift put on earth just for you, and you have no idea what you did to deserve something so wonderful."

Dylan smiled at the image. "Yeah, that's as good a de-scription as any. But she doesn't feel the same way—at least not yet—so I'd appreciate it if you didn't say any-thing in front of her."

"My lips are sealed. But if you have any sense, you won't let her get away, not if you really love her."

"I'm working on it, Dad, trust me. But it's compli-cated."

"Humph. Young people like to say that, but most of life is pretty straightforward, if you want it to be. Just a matter of sorting out what's really important and let-ting the rest be."

"Maybe that's what she's still figuring out. Or maybe she already has, and I didn't make the cut."

"Don't count yourself out yet. She's here, isn't she?"

"She's here because I bribed her with a home-cooked meal."

"Maybe, maybe not. But if you care for her like I think you do, you won't give up on her."

"I won't." She was the first thing he thought of in the morning, and the last thing he thought of at night. Hell, he probably spent most of his waking hours thinking or daydreaming about her. So no, he wasn't going to give up. He couldn't quit her if he wanted to.

Sam sliced one last tomato, then slid the crimson slices off the cutting board and into the salad bowl. She'd braced herself for the usual social awkwardness, but Adele had kept up such a lively stream of conversation about the ranch and her family that she'd never had a chance to feel nervous. She'd even shared a few of her own happy memories, something she hadn't done in years. Maybe it was being in a kitchen that reminded her of the good times. Her mother, like Dylan's, had been an excellent cook. Or maybe it was just Adele's open and honest manner. Either way, Sam was enjoying her time with the older woman so much she was almost disappointed when she heard footsteps ring out behind her.

"Now you two show up, when everything's already done. That figures."

Turning at Adele's reprimand, Sam spotted what had to be Dylan's siblings. They looked to be a few years younger than him, maybe early twenties. Both were tall and fair like he was, but Seth had his hair cut military-short in contrast to Dylan's messy surfer look. Miranda's was pulled back in a tight ponytail, and her blue eyes were several shades lighter than those of the Turner men. She spoke first, glaring at her brother. "If Seth could tie a knot decently, we'd have been back an hour ago."

"The knot was fine, the rope just frayed," he shot back, reaching around her to open the refrigerator. Pouring a glass of milk, he nodded at Sam. "Well, hello, beautiful. I don't think we've met. I'm Seth."

She blushed at his blatant attempt at a pickup. "Uh, nice to meet you, Seth. I'm Sam."

"And she's here with your brother, so don't get any ideas," his mother warned. "I won't have you two fighting over her at dinner."

"I'm not really with him—"

"Yes, she is." Dylan came down the stairway at the

back of the kitchen and narrowed his eyes at Seth. "She most definitely is."

Sam opened her mouth to argue, but Dylan's mother shook her head, obviously trying to avoid a confrontation between the two brothers. Why on earth she thought they'd fight over her, Sam had no idea. Probably another sibling rivalry thing she didn't understand.

Miranda had watched the exchange with interest, as if waiting for it to come to blows.

"Are they always like this?" Sam asked.

"Only when they both want the same thing. You should have seen them battle it out last Thanksgiving over the last piece of pumpkin pie. Brutal."

The last piece of pie? Was that how Dylan saw her? Or was he just posturing to annoy his brother?

"Miranda, don't tease. Seth, please go get your father and tell him dinner is ready. And Dylan, stop glaring at your brother and carry something out to the table." She brushed her hands on the dish towel she'd tied at her waist. "Don't worry, Sam, I promise they can behave when they want to. They just get a bit ornery when they're hungry, always have. Once they've had dinner, they'll turn into real grown-ups and we can have a nice visit."

That blunt prediction proved true, and once everyone had helped themselves to pot roast, mashed potatoes and gravy, salad and biscuits, the mood turned jovial. Of course, it was hard to be anything but happy given the setting. They'd eaten together at the big table on the patio, enjoying the beautiful weather as well as the amazing food.

Seth was seated beside her, and other than a few pointed remarks at his siblings he was a perfect gentleman. Relaxing among the chaos, she almost missed his whispered apology.

"Hey, sorry about before. I didn't mean to make you uncomfortable. If I'd known Dylan and you were together, I wouldn't have tried to hit on you."

She raised an eyebrow, and he laughed. "Okay, maybe I would have. But no worries, I know when to bow out."

"I appreciate the sentiment, but there's nothing going on with us. Not for real." Maybe if she kept saying it, her heart would get the message. Because the more time she spent with Dylan, the harder it was to remember that their relationship was a pretense. But emotions were fickle things, and she couldn't allow her feelings, whatever they were, to determine her actions. Yes, some small part of her wanted to pretend this could be her life, that Dylan's family could one day become her family. But that was the lonely little girl inside her talking. The grown woman she had become knew to keep things based in reality.

Seth shook his head and took another bite of pot roast. "Trust me, I know my brother, and the look he gave me says it's real, at least on his part."

Not wanting to start an argument, Sam turned her attention to the remaining food on her plate, half listening to the boisterous conversation flowing around her. Miranda was still contending that Seth hadn't tied a gate shut properly, and Seth was protesting his innocence while Dylan and their parents weighed in on the various merits of the case. Then the topic turned to upcoming events, and the Outdoor Days Festival.

"Will you be competing in any of the events there, Sam?" the eldest Turner asked as he snagged a second helping of potatoes.

"No, I'll be on duty, actually. The FWC will be providing security, as well as helping to run some of the outdoor-type events—the fishing competition, archery and such."

Dylan looked up from his meal and gazed down the table at the rest of the family. "Sam's boss is going to be there, as well, and he's expecting to see that she's becoming a trusted member of the community. I'm hoping you all will make a point of showing your support while you're there."

"Of course we will, won't we, Ken?" At his nod of agreement, Adele smiled encouragingly at Sam. "It's wonderful to have you here, working to protect the environment. And I'm sure everyone else feels the same way. I know small towns like Paradise, and rural areas like we live in, are so tightly knit that they seem closed off. But I like to think we're a pretty friendly group, all in all."

"I can definitely say I've felt welcome today, so thank you." Not everyone would be as easy to win over as the Turner family, but their open warmth today was definitely a much-needed shot of encouragement.

"You are welcome," Ken stated emphatically. "Any time. And we hope you and Dylan will come and visit often."

"Well, I don't know—"

"We won't take no for an answer," Adele interjected. "I know you're busy right now, with everything going on with the new job, but once things settle down we'll expect you for Sunday dinner on a regular basis. Any friend of Dylan's is a friend of ours."

Sam couldn't help but notice the extra emphasis the woman had put on the word "friend," no doubt insinuating she thought their relationship went beyond the platonic. There was no point in arguing; the more she protested, the more they'd think there was something to hide. If Dylan was a smooth operator, he'd learned it from his parents. So she plastered a smile on her face and said the only thing she could say. "Thank you. I'd love to come back." Which was, she realized, the truth.

Chapter Twelve

Dylan dried the last pan, stacking it neatly in the cupboard when he was done. "Thanks for dinner, Mom. It was amazing, as always."

His mother hugged him hard. "Thank you for coming. It's been too long."

Ah, guilt. The secret weapon of mothers everywhere. "I know. I'll try to get back sooner this time."

"You do that. And bring Sam with you."

He winced. "Mom, I told you, we're not really dating. This is just a temporary thing."

She gave him her famous "don't argue with me" look and he closed his mouth. There was no winning when she got that look on her face. "Dylan Alexander Turner, don't you lie to me."

What? "Mom, I'm not lying about anything."

"Then you admit you're in love with that girl?"

Love, the word he'd been avoiding. Yes, he cared for

her. And he wanted to be with her, in every way. Especially the biblical way. But that was about lust, and friendship and fun, and—

"Dylan?" His mother's gaze bored into his, seeing what he hadn't wanted to see for himself.

"Yes, fine. I'm in love with her." Saying it out loud wasn't as scary as he'd expected. It felt right. "I'm in love with Sam. But that doesn't mean she's in love with me. She's just—"

"She's just confused. She'll figure it out. You just keep being good to her. Actions speak louder than words— that's how you'll win her over."

"Dad said the pretty much the same thing."

"Well, your father is a smart man. Almost as smart as me." She winked, and he felt a rush of gratitude. Both his parents had always supported him, and even now, with this crazy situation, they had his back.

Sam, on the other hand, had lost her mother too young and had a father she hardly saw. But maybe that was something he could help her with. If she was too intimidated to face her old man on her own, he'd go with her.

He waited to bring the idea up until they were in the car, with a well-fed and fully worn-out Toby in the backseat. Sam looked almost as content as the dog. He'd gambled that the relaxed atmosphere of the ranch would have the same effect on her as it did on him, and it seemed he'd won that particular bet. As if feeling his stare, she turned away from where she'd been gazing out the window and smiled.

"Thanks for convincing me to come out here. Your parents are amazing, and so was the food." She stretched back in the seat with a smile. "I had a really nice time."

"Good." He watched her out of the corner of his eye as

he navigated the deserted blacktop that led east toward the coast. "And speaking of parents, I was thinking we could stop at your dad's place on the way back home."

Instantly she stiffened, the tension in the car ratcheting up about a million percent. "I don't think that's a good idea."

"You didn't think going to the ranch today was a good idea, either, but I was right. And I think I'm right about this, too."

"Visiting your family was different...they're normal. My dad is...he's not an easy man to be around."

"I'm not sure anyone would call my family normal, but I get your point. They're comfortable to be around, and I know I'm lucky. But just because things between you and your father have been a bit tense doesn't mean he doesn't miss you. You're still family."

"You don't understand." She crossed her arms tightly against her body.

"Maybe not. But you're the one that said you wanted to try to work things out with him, now that you're living here again. Have you even talked to him since you got here?"

She kept her eyes averted, but he saw her squirm in her seat.

"I didn't think so. So why not tonight? You'll have made the first move, and if it goes terribly we'll just leave. At least you'll have tried."

For several minutes she was silent. Maybe he'd pushed her too hard. It really wasn't his business, except given how he felt about her he couldn't help but want to fix anything broken in her life. He hated seeing her hurt, and more than anything her father's rejection, real or imagined, was causing her pain. If he could help that wound heal, he was going to try. Finally, she sighed and told him where to turn.

"He moved to the mainland when I started college. He says it was because it was a shorter commute to the FWC district office, but I think he just wanted more distance between him and his memories. Now he's still close enough to go into Paradise when he needs to, but far enough away that people don't just stop by."

"Except today."

She frowned. "Yeah. I'm not sure how well that's going to go over."

"You're his daughter. He'll be happy to see you."

Thirty minutes later Dylan wasn't so sure. They'd turned off the highway just before the Paradise Bridge onto a winding dirt road that seemed to get narrower and rougher the farther they went. Branches were brushing against the sides of his truck by the time they turned onto a gravel driveway peppered with potholes. Metal NO TRESPASSING signs were posted prominently in every direction. Sam hadn't been kidding when she said her father had become a virtual hermit. He was half expecting to be greeted with a shotgun blast.

Finally the house itself came into view. The small but sturdy-looking cabin was a simple, one-story affair, painted a deep green that blended in with the surrounding trees. No light shone, but the sounds of a televised baseball game carried through the open windows.

"Ready?"

She nodded but made no move to get out. Toby, however, had none of her misgivings, and after his short nap was bouncing in the backseat, eager to explore. "Think it's okay to take him in with us?"

She shrugged and opened her door. "I don't see why

not. Honestly, Toby's probably more welcome than the rest of us."

Dylan snapped on the dog's leash and let him sniff at the bushes on the edge of the drive while Sam slowly climbed down from the truck and looked up at the house.

"Well, we're here. Might as well go in. But remember, I told you so."

Sam knocked on the door and waited, a false smile on her face. The last thing she wanted to do was have Dylan witness an awkward encounter with her father, especially after seeing how supportive his family had been. Not only of him, but of her, too. They'd made her feel more at home in a few hours than she'd ever felt in her father's lonely hideout in the woods. But Dylan was right—if she wanted things to change, she needed to make the first move. Her father certainly wouldn't, not if the last decade was any indication.

Footsteps and then the sound of a lock turning signaled an answer to her knock. Just as the door started to open, Dylan reached out and gripped her hand, giving her a comforting squeeze of support. Having him at her side shouldn't matter; she had always been strong enough on her own to face whatever came her way. But she couldn't deny that having his support made her stand a little straighter as she prepared to face the one person who still made her feel small.

"Hey, Dad."

Her father stood ramrod-straight, his gray hair and leathered skin the only concessions to his age. He was still trim, with the same lean and muscular build he'd had back when he was a young recruit himself. He wore a polo shirt and khaki shorts and had shaved recently, as if he were expecting visitors or intended to go out. But he didn't go out, not if he didn't have to, and certainly not to socialize. He was dressed neatly because he believed that anything worth doing was worth doing well, even if it was just getting dressed in the morning.

"Sam? What are you doing here? You should have called first."

Her blood chilled and she was grateful for the warm press of Dylan's hand in her own. No exuberant welcome here. Just the ever present disdain she'd come to expect from the man who had once been her biggest hero.

"I hope this isn't a bad time, but Sam and I were in the area and thought we'd stop by to say hello." Dylan's words were as easygoing as ever, but she could feel the sudden tension in his grip. She'd tried to warn him, but even she'd expected a slightly warmer greeting.

"And you are?"

"Dylan Turner, sir. I'm the director of the Paradise Wildlife Rehabilitation Center, and a friend of your daughter's."

"Dad, are you going to let us in or not?" Somehow, seeing him through Dylan's eyes took some of the fear away. Why had she let him intimidate her for so long? She was a grown woman, and if he wasn't interested in spending time with her, then that was his loss. She wasn't going to beg for his attention, not this time.

His eyebrows raised almost imperceptibly at her tone. No doubt he'd expected her to scramble to justify herself, and if Dylan hadn't been there she might have done just that. But this time his behavior wasn't just hurtful, it was embarrassing. Perhaps realizing this, he opened the door and waved them inside.

The cabin's interior was as bland as the exterior. Bare

walls and a total lack of personal touches made the place look more like a rental cabin than a home. The only signs of occupancy were a stout bookcase stuffed with the latest true crime novels and a half-empty glass of amber liquid. Good scotch was the one vice her father allowed himself, and even then only a single glass. There was no chance of her father, the ultimate control freak, ever giving in to a good binge. No, he had too much pride for that.

"So, how have you been, Dad?"

He grunted and lowered himself into a leather wing-back chair near the empty fireplace. "Just fine. How about you? Shouldn't you be working today?"

She managed to keep from rolling her eyes, but just barely. "Dad, I've got the day off. Even us newbies don't have to work seven days a week."

"Maybe not, but it doesn't hurt to put in some extra hours. If not on the job, then on the range, or out in the fields sharpening your skills."

Seriously? She started to defend herself, but Dylan beat her to it.

"Actually, we were out at the range just the other night, and I have to say, your daughter is quite the marksman. She had the whole place in awe of her."

"Well…that is good to hear. But that doesn't mean you can rest on your laurels. Dedication, that's what it takes. Especially for a—"

"A woman. I know. And I am dedicated. I'm working my butt off, in fact. But I'm also trying to make a life outside of work, with friends and family. We had a lovely visit with Dylan's family and thought it would be nice to see you, too. But if we were wrong about that, we can leave."

Her father stroked Toby, who had settled at his feet,

and stared at her as if seeing her for the first time. No doubt he was wondering where his obedient, timid daughter had gone to. Well, tough. She'd wasted enough time trying to please him.

"I was just pointing out that you have more obstacles in front of you than if you were a man. But if you think you have the time to waste on pleasure trips around the countryside—"

"You know what? You're right. This is a waste of time, but it's certainly no pleasure. There hasn't been anything resembling pleasure, or fun, or love in this family since Mom died." After years of being dammed up behind polite silences, the words finally poured from her mouth. "I don't know why you can't love me the way you loved her, or why you hole up here away from anyone that ever gave a damn about you, but I'm done trying to figure it out. Like you said, I've got my work cut out for me if I'm going to make it as a wildlife officer, and there's no point in wasting precious time pretending we're still a family."

For once her father looked shaken. "Listen here, young lady. I don't know what's gotten into you, but you and I are blood, no matter what you think."

"Please, we haven't been a family since Mom died and you sent me away. I don't know why I thought moving here would change that. My mistake." She stood, shaking as the adrenaline shot through her veins. "One I don't intend to repeat. Goodbye, Dad. Have a nice life. Or whatever you call this…existence…that you've created for yourself. Honestly, sometimes I think you might as well have died with her."

She left before he could say anything to stop her, not that she thought he would. Vision blurring, she nearly tripped going down the stairs. Only then did she realize she was crying, and that got her mad all over again. He didn't deserve her tears, and now Dylan was going to think she was some kind of crybaby. Making for the car, she refused to turn around; no way would she let her father see her tears. Behind her, a door slammed shut, the sound a final note to end her childhood. From now on she was on her own.

Dylan jogged after Sam, practically dragging Toby, who couldn't figure out why they were leaving so soon. At least one of them had enjoyed their visit. Of course, Sam's father had been nice to the dog, which was more than could be said for his treatment of his own daughter. How could anyone be so cold and closed off to their own flesh and blood? Dylan and his parents had certainly had their rocky moments, particularly when he'd been a headstrong teen with more ego than brains, but there had always been an underpinning of love to soften any harsh words.

Between Sam and her father there was only mistrust and hurt feelings. On both sides. He'd seen the shock and sorrow on the old man's face when Sam stalked out. There was more than the harsh exterior he'd shown them, but that didn't excuse the way he'd treated Sam. She deserved way better, and anyone who didn't realize how special she was didn't deserve her in their life.

Sam was standing at the side of his truck, her hand on the door handle, waiting for him to unlock it. Gently, he laid a hand on her shoulder, not wanting to push too hard, but needing her to know he was there for her. "I'm sorry. You were right. I shouldn't have pushed you to come here."

She laughed, the sound brittle in the deepening night. "Yeah, well, you couldn't have known."

"I could have listened better. I should have let you explain, rather than thinking everything would be okay."

"I didn't want to explain. I guess maybe I was hoping you were right and that he'd just be happy to see me, the way your parents were happy to see you." She swiped at her face, but he'd already seen the tear tracks. "So I can't blame you. You didn't know what you were getting into, but I should have."

He wanted to take her in his arms, to show her how much she meant to him, but his gut told him this wasn't the time. Even if she let him, he'd be taking advantage of her fragile state. As desperate as he was becoming, even he wouldn't stoop that low. Instead, he unlocked the door and held it open for her and then Toby, who hopped right up into her lap. Might as well let him stay there; if Sam couldn't allow herself to accept comfort from Dylan, the dog was the next best thing.

As they drove, a light rain started to fall, blurring the scenery and erasing the outside world. Inside the car, Sam's breathing was regular—she'd stopped crying at least. But the hurt was still there, under the surface, the way it probably always had been. If this was the kind of treatment she'd grown up with, no wonder she was so hesitant to trust other people. He'd worked with orphaned and abused animals enough to know that emotional trauma could cause more damage than any physical injury.

The one man she should have been able to rely on had utterly failed her. Her mother's death must have been crushing, but at least she hadn't left her daughter on purpose. It would have been a terrible loss, but not a rejection. Her father's treatment, on the other hand, had to feel personal. It was obvious she'd never be able to live up to whatever warped standards he held for her. And equally obvious that until tonight she'd carried that burden as her due.

"You know he's wrong, don't you?" Hearing her father cut her down was bad, but her believing it—that would be unbearable.

"About what?" Her voice was void of emotion, as if she'd emptied herself out there in the cabin and had no reserves to carry her home.

"About everything. About you. You're amazing, and not just at your job. You're an incredible person, and if he can't see that, it's his problem, not yours."

She didn't say anything, just buried her head in the dog's soft fur.

"Hell, even those good old boys at the shooting range admired you. And you've got all the volunteers at the rehab center eating out of your hand. Not to mention the animals. You're caring, and smart, and brave as hell."

"And yet I was too chicken to face my father. If you hadn't insisted we go, I don't know when I would have gotten up the nerve to head over there."

"For good reason." Dylan fisted his hands on the steering wheel. He hated that he was the one that had pushed her into this, but he was also damn proud of how she'd handled herself. "But you did go. And when he got out of line you stood up for yourself, and let him know he was out of line. That took guts."

"Then how come I'm still shaking?" She held out a trembling hand and a piece of his heart cracked.

Checking his mirrors, he pulled the truck to the side of the road and flicked on the emergency lights before unbuckling her seat belt and pulling her into his arms, dog and all.

"Because you had to be stronger than you knew you could be, and your body isn't happy about it. But you did it, you faced him. You said what you've probably been wanting to say for a long time, and you left with your head held high. I'm sorry you had to go through it, but I'm glad you didn't have to do it alone."

If he had his way, she'd never be alone again, not in the way she had been since her mother died. Stroking her hair, he forced his hands to stay gentle, to give comfort rather than take it. This wasn't about his needs; it was about her. And yet, he couldn't just ignore how he felt.

"I'm going to be here for you, in whatever way you'll let me."

She stiffened in his arms, pulling back so they were face to face. "Dylan, I can't—"

He laid a finger on her lips, quieting her. "I know. You haven't had a lot of good experiences with love or with people being there for you. So I'm not going to push."

She nodded, and he moved his finger off her mouth, stroking the silken softness of her cheek. "But I'm not going to let you down, and I'm not going away. When you're ready, I'll be here."

She blinked once, and then slowly moved back to her own seat, untangling her limbs from his. Sighing, she shifted Toby in her lap and refastened her seat belt. Obviously the moment was over.

"I mean it, Sam. I'm not going away. I care for you, and I think that if you let yourself, you could care, too. I'm not your father, damn it. You can trust me."

"Maybe. But I can't think about that now. Let's just stick to the initial agreement."

Frustration ate a hole in his gut. "In other words, we're back to pretending we're dating when we're in public, and when we're in private, pretending we don't have feelings for each other at all." This whole situation was getting more insane by the minute. Why had he ever agreed to this?

"No, I'm saying we shouldn't see each other in private at all."

Chapter Thirteen

Dylan hefted the picnic basket with one hand and shaded his eyes with the other, scoping out the scenic park. Children were playing on the playground while their mothers chatted in the shade. Exercisers of all ages and speeds looped around on the jogging path that circled the park, and on the far side an enthusiastic crowd cheered on a local Little League team. Sam had wanted public, and this was about as public as you could get, short of putting up an ad in the weekly gazette.

He'd just retrieved a folded quilt from the backseat when Sam pulled into the parking spot next to him. Locking up, a habit he hadn't kicked since his time in Boston, he waited for her. She was in a pair of jeans that molded to her body like a second skin and a red T-shirt that had his libido surging like a renegade bull charging a matador's crimson cape. He wanted to scoop her up, put her in his truck and take her somewhere private. Very private.

But this was what she'd insisted on, somewhere they could be seen together, where he could introduce her to more of the community in a casual way. It was the perfect plan. And the exact opposite of what he wanted.

"This looks perfect. Great choice."

"Yeah." He tried to sound enthusiastic and failed utterly.

"Anything wrong?"

Other than him being half in love with a woman who wanted nothing but a businesslike relationship? "Nothing. Let me get Toby and we'll find a place to put our stuff."

At the sound of his name, Toby started up his beagle bellow, making sure Sam and everyone else in the park knew he was there.

"I'm coming, you crazy creature. Just a second." Except, with the picnic basket in one hand and the queen-size quilt in the other, he didn't have a hand left for the leash.

"I'll get him." Sam stepped around to open the passenger door and was greeted by twenty pounds of licking, panting and wagging beagle. "Well, he's certainly happy to see me," she managed between doggy kisses.

"He's not the only one," Dylan muttered. Great, now he was jealous of his dog.

"What was that?" Sam had Toby's leash wrapped around her hand in an attempt to control the eager animal.

"Nothing. I probably shouldn't have brought him, but he started whining, and—"

"And you're a big softy and couldn't leave him behind."

"Pretty much, yeah."

She led the way toward the middle of an open field,

her athletic stride a perfect match for his. "I don't blame you. Poor Toby's had a rough time, and he deserves a picnic just as much as we do. I'm glad you brought him."

He sent a mental thank-you to Toby for earning him a few brownie points with Sam.

"Is this spot okay?"

She'd stopped in the dead center of the park, in full view of anyone and everyone. "As good as anywhere." He set the picnic basket down and unfolded the old quilt, flapping it open and letting it settle to the ground. "I almost forgot, I've got a tie-out stake in the truck for Toby, I'll run get it. Feel free to dig in to the food if you want."

It only took him a few minutes to retrieve the hardware, but by the time he returned Sam was already tossing Toby one of the treats he'd packed. He watched as Toby scarfed it down, then stopped in disbelief when the dog rolled over at Sam's command. "How did you get him to do that?"

She shrugged and tossed the dog another treat. "I didn't, really. I'd already had him sit and lie down, so I thought I'd try it. His previous owner must have trained him to do it. I wonder if he knows any other tricks."

"Well, I can tell you he knows how to get into a closed trash can, and how to open the pantry door to get to his treats."

"Oh, no!"

"Oh, yes. I had to buy a different trash can, and the pantry now has a lock on it. I'd always heard beagles would eat anything, and he pretty much proves it."

"Speaking of food, I'm starving. Think he'll settle down and let us eat?"

"I packed him one of his chew bones, so we should be fine."

"Ah, Toby gets his own picnic." She gave his arm a squeeze, a friendly gesture that had him feeling decidedly more than friendly. "You really are a nice guy."

He'd get the darn dog a crateful of bones if it would help. "Why don't you unpack the food while I deal with the dog?"

"Deal."

The tie-out stake he'd purchased online was like a giant corkscrew, and it worked in a similar manner. Once he'd twisted it into the ground to anchor it, he clipped Toby's leash into the attached carabiner and then gave it a pull. Only when he was sure it would hold did he let go of the leash, leaving the dog to happily gnaw on the rawhide Sam had pulled from the basket.

Sam was kneeling on the blanket, where she'd set out a plate for each of them. "I see sandwiches, potato salad, fruit salad and brownies. Are you more domestic than I thought, or did you pick this up from somewhere?"

"A little of both." He snagged a sandwich and offered her half. "I made the brownies—from scratch. One of the few things I know how to make. The rest I picked up at the diner."

"Points for honesty, and bonus points for baking the brownies. I would not have expected that."

"My mom taught all us kids to cook at various times, but living on my own I've forgotten a lot of it. It's not much fun cooking for one. But brownies, those are a necessity."

"A man after my own heart."

Where did that come from? Other than the obvious— he really was the ideal man. But no matter how much she liked him, and the more she was around him the more she liked him, she needed to remember that their relationship was nothing but an illusion, a bit of misdirection to help smooth her entry into Paradise's inner circle. Of course, when she'd suggested the idea, she hadn't known how hard it was going to be to keep her own emotions in check. Thankfully, he seemed to take the quip as a lighthearted compliment, not a confession of her growing feelings for him.

Grabbing a sandwich and some fruit, she forced herself to think of something other than Dylan and the conflicted feelings that surfaced whenever they were together. Instead, she turned her attention to the beauty of their surroundings, letting the tension in her body melt under the heat of the fall sunshine. The sky was almost achingly blue, with a single white cloud, and the temperature was perfect—warm but not hot, with enough of a breeze for them to smell the salt off the ocean. Overhead a hawk circled slowly while squirrels chattered in the trees. It really was a perfect day for a romantic picnic; too bad the romance was all in her head.

Part of her wanted to just confess her confusion and see if he was even still interested in dating for real. But even if he was interested, the timing was all wrong. She couldn't afford any more distractions, and as much as being around him now messed with her head, a relationship would be more than she could handle. Maybe after she had secured her job and proven herself, she could afford to have something more than a fake boyfriend. But by then he'd probably be ready to move on. Men like Dylan weren't the settle-down types and she wouldn't settle for a fling.

Even if it did sound pretty appealing right now. Of course that was her hormones talking, not her heart. And

make no mistake, Dylan was more than capable of breaking her heart. But only if she let him. Which was why
she had to keep things like they were: all pretense and
no chance of getting hurt.

"Is the food okay? I thought about getting something
fancier, but I didn't want it to look staged."

"It's fine." She glanced around. "Do you think it's
working?"

"Are you kidding? See that group of women over
there?" He pointed to a cluster of tracksuit-clad seniors
near the water fountain. "They were walking on the trail,
but stopped after they saw us. They've been standing
there, watching, ever since."

"Seriously?"

He forked a second helping of potato salad onto his
plate and nodded. "Cross my heart. They're the matrons
of the Paradise gossip brigade. That's Mrs. Rosenberg
there in the pink, leopard-print jacket. She makes it her
business to know everything worth knowing. She won't
share anything malicious—she's too kindhearted for
that—but a lover's tryst? That would get top billing."

Sam managed to finish her suddenly tasteless sandwich out of a sense of politeness, but her appetite was
gone. She never should have suggested such a public
venue. Yes, she wanted to make sure their so-called relationship became public knowledge, but she'd anticipated
something a bit more subtle. Maybe a T-ball mom noticing and then casually mentioning it to her hairdresser,
not a passel of self-appointed town criers circling like
sharks on a chum line.

Dylan's appetite, however, seemed unaffected. He
wolfed down two sandwiches, both kinds of salad and a
brownie. Part of her wanted to be annoyed. How could

he be so calm when their privacy was being so blatantly invaded? But of course, that was the whole point. Why should he be bothered by the exact thing they'd set out to create?

Either way, she wasn't going to be able to keep eating as if nothing was going on; the little bit she'd had felt like a lead anchor in her stomach. Laying down on the blanket, she propped herself on one arm and tried to at least pretend she was enjoying herself. "At least it's a pretty day."

"Hmm?" Dylan swallowed the last of what she was pretty sure was his third brownie. How men could eat so much and not gain weight was a mystery. "Sorry, what were you saying?"

"Nothing, really. Just commenting on the weather."

He arched an eyebrow, looking down at her with feigned offense. "Wow. Has it really come to that, small talk about the weather?"

She bristled. "Hey, at least I'm trying to make conversation, not just stuffing my face."

"Whoa, slow down. I was just teasing. And the last time I checked, eating was considered a socially acceptable activity for a picnic." As if to emphasize his point, he grabbed a strawberry off her plate and plopped it into his mouth whole, his eyes daring her to say more.

"Sorry. You're right." Which was seriously annoying. "I'm just a bit on edge, I guess."

"Because of me?" He lowered himself down, propping his head on one hand in the mirror image of her position.

He was too close, so close she could smell the crisp scent of his soap, so close she could feel the whisper of his breath on her skin. Unable to speak, she shook her head, willing him to understand.

"Because of our audience?" His free hand brushed a strand of hair from her face, lingering at the nape of her neck.

She managed the barest of nods, unable to look away as he leaned in closer.

"Then let's make sure they get their money's worth."

And then his lips were on hers, as gentle as the brush of butterfly wings. A chaste, strawberry-flavored kiss, one that hinted rather than demanded. A whimper of frustration slipped out—she wanted, no, she *needed* more. Tentatively, she brushed the seam of his lips with her tongue, and then he was kissing her for real, and she couldn't think of a single reason to stop him.

Dylan had only intended an innocent peck, something to cement their status in the minds of the public. He'd half expected Sam to push him away, or to roll her eyes in frustration. Instead, she'd deepened the kiss, teasing him with her tongue. But it had been her whimper that had broken him, and he'd taken her mouth the way he'd wanted to since their very first meeting in the woods. Never had a kiss felt so right, or his body reacted so quickly. Shifting his weight, he braced himself over her, changing the angle to better explore the sweetness of her mouth. Urging him on, she gripped his shoulders, pulling him more fully against her.

He was so intent on Sam he barely registered the shadow that suddenly blocked out the warm sun. But there was no ignoring the wet tongue on the back of his neck. "Toby! Get!" He reached up to push the beagle away, but Sam was already squirming out from underneath him. Sitting up, she smoothed her shirt and darted a glance toward their audience. He followed her gaze to where Mrs. Rosenberg was giving them a thumbs-up. So much for subtlety.

"I guess we impressed them." That he could speak at all after such a rush of hormones and emotion was a credit.

"You shouldn't have done that," she hissed under her breath, flashing the old ladies a tight smile. "We had an agreement. Nothing physical. Kissing wasn't part of the deal."

"Whoa, slow down there. Don't pin this all on me. You kissed me right back. You wanted that every bit as much as I did. You're just too damn scared to admit it."

"I'm not scared, I'm angry!"

"At me, or yourself?" She glared, and started packing up the food, shoving things into baskets with hard, jerking motions. He'd hit a nerve, even if she wouldn't admit it. "You can't keep pretending you don't have feelings for me just because you're afraid of being hurt."

"Who says I'm pretending? Did it ever occur to you that I'm just honestly not interested in you that way?"

"That kiss says you are."

"You can't make decisions based on a kiss. That's just lust talking."

"No, it isn't." He scrubbed a hand through his hair. "Yes, I'm attracted to you, but it's more than that. The truth is, I'm head over heels in love with you. Do you know what that means?"

"That you're delusional? That you've let your imagination run away with you, so that what was supposed to be a fake relationship somehow feels real?

"No. It means you have all the power here."

Her hands stilled, the half-folded blanket hanging limp. At least now he had her attention.

"Don't you see that you're so afraid of being rejected that you're willing to walk away from something wonderful? If you do that, if you deny yourself the chance to see what this could be, you'll be the one doing the same thing you've been so angry with your father for."

"You have no idea what you're talking about."

"Don't I?" Damn it, he was tired of skirting the issue. "Your father shut down his heart when he lost your mother. It wasn't right, but I guess he just was too scared to risk loving anyone else, even you, the way he'd loved her. He was afraid of being hurt again. And you're doing exactly the same thing, pushing away the one who loves you because you're terrified I might not stick around."

"So what if I am?" Her voice broke, and he knew he was the cause. But it was too late to take it all back now. "Don't I have a right to protect myself? I've lost too much. I can't handle risking everything, not again."

"See, here's the part you don't get. You *can* handle it— you're strong enough to handle anything. You survived your mother's death, and your father's absence, and the loss of the only home you'd ever known. No, you didn't just survive, you thrived. You pushed yourself to be the best at everything, and you succeeded." He smiled, because the pain couldn't erase the love he felt for her. "Even if someone breaks your heart one day, you're always going to bc come out on top, because that's just who you are. But until you can believe that, I guess I don't stand a chance. So hey, you win. You keep your heart all safe and sound, bound up where no one can reach it." His hand shook at the truth of what he was saying. "And I lose. Because I'm the stupid schmuck who can't seem to help loving you."

Sam stood, the remnants of their picnic around her,

the sun shining on the tears that had slipped down her cheeks. How could one woman be both so perfect, and so broken, all at the same time? And why did he feel like a heel for making her cry, when his only crime was loving her? Wasn't love supposed to be a good thing? They should be walking on air, celebrating that they'd each found someone to care about. Instead, his gut was a pit of anger and frustration and she looked like he'd kicked her favorite puppy.

Maybe he should have waited longer to confess his feelings, but if not now, when? Right after a smoking-hot kiss had seemed like the obvious choice. But with Sam, he was beginning to realize that nothing was simple or obvious. He'd dealt with complex problems all his life, on the ranch, in school and on the job. But Sam's issues were something he couldn't reason or think all the way through. She had to do that on her own. All he could do was stick around and be there for her while she did it.

The question was, would she let him?

Sam couldn't believe she was crying again. Twice in two days, after years without shedding a single tear. What had happened to her?

Oh, yeah—Dylan had happened. He'd slammed into her life without warning, and now every way she turned he was there, poking and prodding all the sore places she'd learned to ignore. He made her feel things again. And that scared the hell out of her.

And for good reason! Look at what happened when she let her guard down—she was a basket case. Crying in public, making a scene in front of every gossip in town, just days before her boss would be arriving to evaluate her. So much for convincing everyone they were a couple.

It was pretty clear right now that any hope of having people accept her because of him was long gone. Once word got out that they'd been seen fighting, everyone would start choosing sides. And if it was a choice between the town golden boy or the chick with a badge who had the added bonus of a hermit for a father, she knew who she'd bet on.

"Sam, say something. Tell me you'll give us a chance."

She shook her head, her mind reeling with everything he'd said. He was in love with her? How was that possible? He'd seen her flaws, how messed up she was. She couldn't trust, couldn't love, not the way he wanted her to. And just because she was afraid of getting hurt, although, yeah, she was pretty much terrified of that. But even worse was the idea of hurting him. She had to make him see that. He needed to understand that she wasn't good for him, not now, not ever.

"It's not about giving anyone a chance, Dylan. It's about doing the right thing, and acting like a grown-up, not a love-struck teenager. This is real life, not some fairy tale."

"Don't you think I know that? My love for you is real, and so are your feelings, even if you won't admit you have them."

"A relationship with me is a recipe for disaster." She swiped her hair out of her face and straightened, needing him to see she wasn't going to back down. "I don't want to put either of us through that. Surely you can see that it's better to just stay friends. Friends, I can do."

"Is this because you think I'll abandon you one day, like your father? Because I'm not him, Sam. I'm nothing like him."

"I know, but what if I am?" she shouted, her voice

cracking along with her heart. "What if I end up as cold and hard as he is?"

Dylan's eyes widened in shock. "How can you say that?"

"Because it's the truth. He wasn't always this way. He used to be caring and fun. He was an amazing father, until one day he wasn't. He just shut down, and I was left on the outside. I don't want to do that to you." As she said the words, a load lifted. She'd harbored this secret fear for so long, longer than she could remember. Admitting it took some of the pain away, and gave her a little room to breathe. "That's why I can't do this with you. I refuse to hurt anyone the way he hurt me."

"Don't you think that's my decision to make? I'm a big boy, and I can take care of myself."

She shook her head, even as more tears fell. "No. I'm sorry."

Dylan growled in frustration, looking like he wanted to throw something. Honestly, she wouldn't mind a physical outlet for some of the emotion coursing through her veins, but pitching the picnic basket across the park wouldn't do her reputation any favors. Instead she refolded the blanket she'd dropped, stacking it on top of the basket.

"So, where does that leave us now?" He sounded lost, reaffirming her decision. She'd already caused him pain; how much worse would the damage be if they'd really been in a relationship?

"We could go back to how things were. The original agreement."

"No, we can't."

She stopped, the finality in his voice sending waves of panic down her spine. "What? Are you worried everyone will hear about—" she gestured between them "—all of this? Because I think we could play it off as a lovers' spat."

"No. I mean I can't. Pretending to be a couple when we could have the real thing, that's too hard. If we're going to keep seeing each other, you have to be honest with me about your feelings. We can go slow, but I can't go backward. I can't forget what it felt like to kiss you, or how you feel in my arms."

Pain, as real as if she'd been stabbed with a knife, sliced through her. He was determined to make this as hard as possible for her, but like he had said, she was strong. "If that's what you want—"

"No, it's not what I want. None of this is what I want." His eyes shimmered with pent-up emotion, threatening to drown them both if she didn't hold strong.

Digging her nails into her palms, she nodded, and did what she'd known was coming, from that first dinner. She left. One foot in front of the other, gaze straight ahead, her breaths coming with forced rhythm. All she had to do was keep moving. Across the lawn to her car, then to her apartment, and then on with her life. Just one impossible step after the other.

Chapter Fourteen

Sam threw her weight behind the shovel, digging deep into the layer of wood chips that lined the stall. Intrigued, the fawn she'd helped rescue watched from the other side of the fence, enjoying some outdoor time while Sam cleaned out the soiled bedding and replaced it with fresh.

Sweat trickled down her neck, an hour of hard work no match for the slight breeze that barely stirred the air today. She'd gotten a lot done, though, working out her bad mood with hard manual labor.

It usually helped, at least for a little while. She'd been coming to the rehab center daily, as she'd originally promised, despite the ending of her arrangement with Dylan. He'd been startled the first time he saw her, but had wisely kept his mouth shut. She wasn't the kind of person to back out of a contract or change the terms midstream, even if he wasn't sticking to his end of the bargain.

Over the past few days she'd gone from upset, to angry, to empty inside. Only to have the whole cycle start over again every time she saw him. Or thought about him. Or just at random times. But seeing him was the worst. He seemed to look right through her now, as if he couldn't stand the sight of her. Hard to believe that a few days ago he'd professed his love. It seems his feelings weren't quite as deep as he'd made them out to be.

No, she'd been right to keep things from progressing. If he could turn his emotions off so quickly, there couldn't have been much there in the first place. Which hurt more than she'd expected it to. The strength of her own feelings had also surprised her. She'd cried most of Sunday night, off and on, and had been on the verge of changing her mind Monday morning. Which just made Dylan's rapid about-face all the harder to take.

Angry all over again, she started scooping clean shavings into the now empty pen. Possibly with more force than was strictly necessary, but the animals didn't care. Once she was done with this chore, she needed to check next week's schedule and make sure they'd taken her off the rotation. The Outdoor Days Festival was this weekend and that was the end of her commitment.

What happened after that was anyone's guess. Since the incident at the park, she hadn't spent much time in town. Between mornings volunteering at the rehab center, long days patrolling huge swaths of Palmetto County wilderness and evenings staking out the scene of the poaching, she hadn't had the time to socialize. Or maybe she was just too chicken to find out what the latest gossip was. Surely word of their breakup had spread by now, and if people decided to turn on her she'd be out of a job by this time next week.

And probably out of a home, as well—she'd have no reason to stay if her job was gone. Her relationship with her father certainly was nothing to stick around for, and Dylan had made clear that he wasn't interested in being her friend. All or nothing, that's what he'd said, and his actions this week showed he'd meant it.

Satisfied the enclosure was ready, she unlatched the gate to the outer area and let the fawn back into his temporary home. Kicking his heels up in the thick wood shavings, the deer made a circle of the pen, then scampered over to butt his head against her.

"He's getting a bit big for his britches, isn't he?" Donna, one of the volunteers she'd gotten to know over the last few weeks, leaned on the fence watching the orphan's antics. "It's good he's being released soon. He really needs more space."

Sam let herself out of the pen, rubbing the sore spot on her hip where the fawn's head had connected. "He's being released?"

Donna nodded. "Any day now. He's ready, and if we keep him much longer he'll end up too tame."

"I know you're right, but I'm going to miss him."

"Isn't this your last week, anyway?"

She nodded, feeling a heaviness settle over her. "Good point. I guess I hadn't really thought about it." She straightened, pushing off the fence. "In fact, I'd better go inside and make sure they remembered to take me off the schedule."

Donna grimaced. "You might want to just call in later and check. Dylan's at his desk and he's in rare form today. If he doesn't lighten up, I'm thinking of calling in sick tomorrow."

"He's been in a bad mood? I thought it was just me he was acting that way with."

"Not even close. He's been biting off everyone's heads all week. I'm telling you, you don't want to go in there."

"Thanks for the warning, but I'll take my chances." She wasn't going to let him scare her away. She'd handled far worse than a grumpy surfer in her lifetime. She was the one doing him a favor, working here. Heck, they all were. The least he could do was be civil. He probably was just upset she'd turned him down. But a bruised ego didn't give him a right to go around acting like a wounded bear. She had just as much reason to be upset as he did, and she was holding it together just fine.

Okay, maybe she wasn't quite fine. But she was the one on the verge of losing everything that meant anything to her. What had he lost, a few dates? Because no matter what he said about love, and standing by her, chances were it never would have been more than that. So if anyone was going to get to be angry, it was her. And if he pulled any crap, she was going to tell him so to his face.

If he thought she was tough before, he hadn't seen anything yet.

Dylan quickly typed out a response to yet another email, his fingers tapping out an angry rhythm. He was sick and tired of schmoozing donors, trying to squeeze another few bucks out of them every time something broke or they got another injured animal in. He was sick of all of it, really. All he did was work, and what did he have to show for it? Nothing.

He hit Send and heard the door open behind him. "Donna, I thought I said I needed a bit of peace and quiet in here? I can't get everything done if I'm being interrupted every five minutes."

"Wow, Donna was right. You really are acting like a jerk."

Dylan spun around in his chair, whacking his knee on the open desk drawer. Pain, in his knee and his heart, took his breath away. Every time he saw Sam, it was like a knife was being twisted, reopening the wound he didn't know how to heal.

"I'm not acting like anything."

"Fine. I'm just here to check the schedule quick and then I'll get out of your way. But if you want any of your other volunteers to stick around you might want to change your attitude. Donna's ready to mutiny, and I bet she's not the only one."

"So now you're the one giving me lessons in social skills? That's ironic."

She blinked, and he saw hurt in her eyes. "Damn it, Sam, I didn't mean that. I'm sorry."

"You should be. And you should apologize to Donna, too."

"You're right, and I will. I've been acting like a jerk, to you and everyone else." He forced a smile. "Can you forgive me?"

For a second he thought she was going to say no. He wouldn't blame her, either. He knew he'd been out of line, but he just couldn't seem to snap out of it. Seeing her, but not being with her, was killing him. Even now, as she stood there scowling at him, he wanted to beg her for another chance. The only thing stopping him was the memory of her crying. His desire to be with her was at war with his instinct to protect her, even from himself.

She sighed. "Fine, I forgive you. I don't want hard feelings between us."

"Neither do I." That was the last thing he wanted. He offered his hand. "Can we call a truce?"

"Truce." She took his hand, and just that simple touch, the soft skin of her hand in his, was like a jolt of electricity, igniting his need all over again.

She dropped his hand as quickly as she'd taken it, and he wondered if she'd felt it, too. Rubbing her palm on her pants, she looked up at him cautiously. "Does this mean we can go back to being friends?"

He was beginning to hate that word. But he'd tried keeping his distance, towing a hard line, and all it had done was make him miserable and guilty. He'd said he'd help her, and instead he'd made things harder. He couldn't fix everything he'd ruined, and he certainly couldn't help the way he felt about her, but he could be her friend. No matter how much it hurt. "Sure. Friends."

She smiled, and the pain eased just a bit. He'd put up with anything to see that smile. "So, you said something about the schedule?" Maybe she was going to sign on permanently?

"Oh, yeah." She walked over to the counter and picked up a clipboard, flipping to the second page. "I wanted to be sure I wasn't in the rotation after this week. I wouldn't want anyone left in the lurch."

So much for that idea. "No worries, I already checked. You're not scheduled after Friday." Now he wished he'd spent more time with her this week. He only had two more mornings left with her, and he'd wasted the last three avoiding her in hopes that it would make it easier to get over her.

But there was no getting over Sam. She infiltrated

his dreams, she haunted his every waking moment. She didn't have to be in the room to make him want her; he'd want her and love her, even from the ends of the earth. Pushing her away wouldn't change that. He was starting to think nothing would.

Sam cleared her throat, shifting from one foot to the other. "So, have you heard anything around town? About us, I mean?"

"Not really. But I haven't really run into anyone. I've been working late, then going straight home. The only people I've talked to are you and the staff. If there are rumors going around, none of them have come to me, but you heard Donna. I haven't exactly been open to conversation."

"Oh, okay. I was just wondering. I guess I'll see you tomorrow." She nervously nibbled her bottom lip and he gripped the arms of his chair. Every primitive male instinct was pushing him to taste those lips himself, to hold her and make her believe everything was going to be okay. But he wasn't a caveman and he couldn't force her to feel what he felt.

So he would respect her boundaries. He'd let her work through this on her own. And he'd hate every minute of it.

"Yeah, see you tomorrow."

Sam leaned against her kitchen counter, listening to the whirring of the microwave. Dinner from a box, but at least she was home for dinner tonight. She'd given up her evening stakeout—no one had showed and no one was likely to. It wasn't a great hunting spot, and whoever had shot the doe had probably just been driving through when they spotted the deer. A crime of convenience, making it nearly impossible to track down the perpetrators. The only chance she had of solving the case was for someone to turn the poachers in, and so far she hadn't received a single tip.

The microwave beeped, followed quickly by the doorbell ringing. Who on earth could that be? Maybe the landlord needed something, or a neighbor? She pulled out her dinner and set it on the counter to cool, warning Cheesy away from it with a stern look. He was known to steal people food and she didn't want the greedy cat to burn himself while her back was turned.

Hand on the lock, she stopped to look through the peephole. There was a time when her door had been always open, but law enforcement training had ended that habit. Outside, through the distorted view of the glass, she could make out a handful of people. The porch light wasn't bright enough to make out all the faces, but the one in front was definitely Dani.

Opening the door, she stared in bewilderment.

"Hey, Sam! Can we come in?"

"Um, yes. Sure. But...what's going on?"

Dani hefted a bottle of wine. "Girls' night in. We would have called, but I thought it would be more fun to surprise you." She winked. "And I was right. You should see your face." She maneuvered her way past Sam, and gestured to the women following behind. "Sam, meet the girls. My sister Mollie is the one with the bag of snacks, Cassie is the one that looks like she swallowed a watermelon and I think you've met Jillian already. The little munchkin on her shoulder is Jonathan."

"And I'm Jessica, Cassie's sister-in-law," a voice from the back piped up. As the crowd of women moved into the apartment the last in line, a young woman about her own age with a copper-toned complexion and curly, dark hair waved. "My brother Alex sent me to keep an eye on Cassie. He's convinced she's going to go into labor and deliver without him."

Given how pregnant the strawberry blonde standing in her kitchen looked, she couldn't blame him. Catching her alarmed expression, Cassie laughed and rubbed her distended belly. "Don't worry, I promise not to give birth tonight. This is probably my last girls' night for a while, and I'm not going to ruin it. Besides, I'm the designated driver. So this baby is staying put until further orders."

"If she says it, you can believe it," Dani assured her as she poured glasses of wine. "Cassie is as stubborn as they come. She'll will that baby out when she's ready, and not a second before."

"Good to know." She took the glass of red wine Dani thrust at her. "But seriously, what are you all doing here? Not that I mind," she added. "But I feel like I'm missing the punch line or something."

Dani clinked her glass with Sam's, then took a large swig of the potent wine. "No punch line. We just thought you might need some company."

Jillian stepped forward and smiled. "We heard about you and Dylan breaking up, and wanted to show our support. I know when Nic and I were having trouble, I couldn't have made it without Cassie and Mollie." She flashed them a look of gratitude, and once again Sam found herself longing for what these women had.

"Us women have to stick together." This was from Mollie, who looked like a younger, more casual version of her sister. In cutoffs and a T-shirt she wasn't at all what Sam'd expected of a famous photographer. "We brought wine, ice cream and pizza. And if that doesn't work, we can always go over there and beat him up for you."

Sam sputtered, spraying wine. Mollie smacked her on the back. "Don't worry, we're not usually violent. Only if you need us to be."

Accepting a napkin from Jessica, who had been putting pizza slices on paper plates, she dabbed at her now sodden shirt. "I think we can probably avoid that. Whose idea was this, anyway?" She turned to Dani, who held up a hand in protest.

"Don't look at me. Jillian made the first call. I came because Mollie did."

Jillian? She turned to the young mother. "But you barely know me!"

The brunette blushed prettily. "I actually can't take credit either. It was Mrs. Rosenberg's idea."

"The old lady at the park? With the crazy glasses? What does she have to do with this?"

Jillian shifted the baby to her other shoulder, patting him rhythmically. "She realized you and Dylan had broken up, or at least had a fight, and thought you might need some female support. She called me, and I called the rest of them. Mrs. Rosenberg wanted to be here herself, but she had a bridge game at the senior center."

Sam paused, mentally picturing the ostentatious octogenarian drinking wine in her living room with the rest of them and felt a giggle bubble up. Before she could stop herself, she was doubled over, laughing and crying at the same time. Alarmed, Cassie levered herself out of a chair and leaned over Sam. "Are you okay?"

Sam nodded, trying to catch her breath. "Oh, my goodness, yes. It's just, I'm not sure if I'm flattered or terrified. One minute I was sitting here by myself, getting ready to eat a frozen dinner. The next I have a tactical team of women on my doorstep ready to cheer me up at all costs."

"Hey, that's what friends do, right?" Dani asked, her mouth full of pizza.

Sam looked around the room. Cassie was next to her, a paper plate balanced on her enormous belly, ready to comfort Sam if she started crying again. Jessica was helping herself to another slice of pizza at the breakfast bar and keeping a watchful eye on Cassie. Mollie sat cross-legged on the floor next to Dani, the two sisters at once so similar and yet so different. Together, these women had taken it upon themselves to come over, unannounced, just to make sure she was okay. No one seemed to expect anything of her, other than her company. They just wanted to hang out, and make sure she was all right. "Yeah, I guess it is."

A year ago, or even a month ago, she wouldn't have been able to say that. Her experience of friendship had been limited to casual nods and the occasional study group. But this was different. This was something tangible, something she instinctively knew she could count on. The kind of friendship she'd read about in books, the kind she'd given up on finding. Somehow what had seemed impossible was now happening, and all she'd had to do was allow them in.

Could it be that simple? All the walls she'd built to protect herself, her heart; had they been keeping out the happiness she'd longed for? She'd let Dani and these amazing women into her life, and they'd made it better. What would happen if she opened up to Dylan, too? Could she find a way to make bridges instead of barriers, and still keep herself whole?

Chapter Fifteen

"I thought I heard you in here."

Sam turned away from the counter where she'd been chopping up vegetables for some of the rehab center's animals. "Just making sure the critters get their dinner."

"I missed you this morning." Dylan's tone was casual, but she felt a bit of a thrill anyway. She had wondered if he would notice her absence.

"Sorry, I got a call before dawn about a lost hiker. We found him, but by the time everything was settled it was already midmorning, so I called and switched shifts."

"No worries. I'm glad everything turned out okay."

She went back to chopping, finding it easier to talk if she didn't have to look him in the eye. Ever since her epiphany the other night when Dani and the girls had come over, she'd been thinking about him and her, and if she was doing the right thing. Was she wrong to keep things platonic between them, or just being practical? How much was fear, and how much was common sense? Part of her wanted to just give up the pretense, to be brave enough to open up and see where things led. But what if that was just her hormones talking? She needed more time, time to think things through and figure out the next step. Except thinking was pretty much impossible when he was standing so close to her. Slicing the zucchini for the tortoises, she nodded. "It did. Two brothers were camping out in the preserve, and during the night one of them went out to use the bathroom but never came back. He'd been gone a while before they called us, as the other brother had fallen back asleep. I was the closest, so first on the scene, but it was Cassie's husband, Alex, that finally found him. Or should I say, Alex's K9 partner, Rex."

"Speaking of them, I heard Cassie was over at your place the other night, right before she had her baby." He leaned against the counter, close enough that she could smell the piney aftershave he wore.

Senses tingling, she tried to focus on his words, and not on how easy it would be to lean in to his hard body. "Oh, yeah. It was crazy. She seemed fine when she left, but I guess she went into labor just a few hours later. She's adorable, too—the baby, I mean. I stopped by the hospital yesterday to see her. But it wasn't just her that came by. There was a whole group—Jillian, Mollie, Dani, and Alex's sister Jessica, who came into town for Outdoor Days this weekend."

"Oh, I haven't met her yet. I'll have to keep an eye out and introduce myself."

A flicker of green-eyed jealousy sparked in Sam's belly. Just because things hadn't worked out between them didn't mean he should be on the prowl for a new woman so soon. Annoyed at him, and more annoyed at herself for caring, her concentration slipped along with the knife in her hand. "Ouch!"

"What happened? Are you okay?"

Blood oozed from a half-inch gash on her left index finger. "I'm fine, I just cut myself a little."

"That's more than a little. Here, let's clean it off and then I'll get the first aid kit." He took hold of her hand and guided her to the sink. Turning the faucet, he held her finger under the cool running water, his body pressed against hers. "Does it hurt?"

"Hmm? Oh, no, not really." She couldn't feel anything but him. Lust had commandeered her nerve endings, leaving no room for something as inconsequential as pain.

"Good." He leaned over her shoulder, peering down at the wound. "I don't think you need stitches, but maybe I should take you over to the hospital just to be sure."

She could feel his breath on her neck, raising chill bumps and stirring her emotions. This was crazy: she was bleeding into the sink and all she could think about was how much she wanted him to kiss her.

"What do you think?"

"About what?"

"Do you want me to take you to the hospital to get that looked at?"

She shook her head, forcing her mind back onto the here and now, not the what-ifs that kept trying to trip her up. "No, just a bandage. Whatever you have in the first aid kit should be fine."

"Okay. Let me see what I can find." He let go of her, and she had to stop herself from pulling him back. This must be the exhaustion talking, making her vulnerable, keeping her from thinking straight. Her new friends had stayed late, and she'd only been in bed a few hours before she'd been woken to search for the missing camper. Tonight she'd get a solid eight hours of sleep and be back to her normal self by the morning.

"This should work." Dylan held up a rectangular bandage and some antibiotic ointment. "Just dry it off and I'll get you patched back up."

She grabbed a paper towel and did as he instructed, holding her finger out for him to take care of. "You know, I'm the one with first aid training, so how come you know so much about this?"

"Will it offend you if I say I learned watching Cassie?"

She chuckled. "So you're saying your training is in veterinary care?"

He grinned. "Don't worry, I promise not to give you a rabies vaccine or make you wear one of those plastic cones on your head."

"Thank goodness."

He wrapped the last bit of adhesive around her finger. "One thing left to do."

"Oh, yeah? What's that?"

"A kiss to make it better." Without waiting for a response from her, he lifted her hand to his mouth, his gaze locked on hers, and gently kissed her bandaged finger. Heat flared in her belly, answering the fire she saw in his eyes.

"Dylan…" She sighed, needing to stop him and yet needing him to never stop. She hesitated, and the choice was taken from her. A chirp from her pocket signaled a call on her work phone. She pulled her hand back and forced herself to step away. "I have to answer this, I'm sorry."

"Fine, but we're not done here."

She answered, listening with mounting anticipation. This was it, the break she'd needed. Running to her purse, she grabbed a pen and her notepad, scrawling down directions and then repeating them to be sure. "Thank you so much. I'm on my way."

Shoving the phone back in her pocket she turned to Dylan. "I've got to go. That was a tip about the poachers—someone spotted them with another deer."

"Wow, that's…great." And it was, in a general kind of way. But unless he was mistaken, it also meant she was about to head off to confront armed poachers. Which wasn't at all what he'd call good news. "So, now what?"

She looked up from her phone, and he saw she'd already pulled up a map of the island. "Now I try to get there before they clean up and dispose of the evidence."

"You don't think you should call in someone else? Backup, maybe?" He'd feel a lot better if she had reinforcements. Maybe an entire squadron of armed guards.

She nodded, her fingers flying over the phone. "I will. But the next closest agent is an hour away. He'll meet me out there when he can."

"You're not going to wait for him?" Fear tightened around his gut like a snake constricting its prey.

"No, I just told you—I can't wait, not if I want to catch them red-handed. In an hour from now, they could have packed everything up and be sitting in front of the television watching a baseball game."

Dylan desperately wished he could believe these idiots had nothing worse on their mind than a game and a beer. "It just doesn't seem safe, that's all."

Her shoulders stiffened, and he swore there was ice in her gaze. "Dylan Turner, I am a trained law enforcement officer. This is my job—it's what I do. You've known that from the minute you met me. If you have a problem with that, you'll have to work it out on your own. I don't have time for this kind of sexist crap."

"Whoa, sexist? Just because I'm just a bit concerned about you running off to confront a bunch of armed criminals doesn't make me sexist!"

She put her hands on her hips and cocked her head. "Oh, really? And I assume you show this same amount of concern for your friend Alex as he goes about his job. Do you follow his patrol car around town to make sure he doesn't get into any trouble? Or do you trust that he has the training, knowledge and skills to handle himself?"

Damn. She was right, except for one thing. "The difference is, I'm not in love with Alex."

She blinked twice, rapidly, but didn't back down. "So, what? I'm supposed to quit my job because you're in love with me and worried I might get hurt?"

It shocked him that there was a tiny part of him that did want that, as illogical as it was. .But he wasn't a caveman, and even if he wanted to lock her away from every sort of danger, he'd never be able to live with himself if he stood between her and her duty. "No." He drew a deep breath, trying to calm the fear that coursed through him. "You love your job, and you've worked hard to get to this point. It's what you were meant to do."

"Thank you."

"But it doesn't mean I have to like it. I'm not going to lie, Sam. I'm scared to death. I was raised to believe that a man protects the people he loves, and you want me to stand here and do nothing, to let you face danger on your own." His fists clenched at his side. "Sam, I don't know how to do that."

"Well, that's too bad." She grabbed her keys and headed for the door, then stopped, spinning to face him. "You know, you've talked a lot about how I'm living in fear, that I'm too scared to trust my feelings for you. And maybe you're right. But you don't get to sit there and lecture me about fear when you're too scared to let me do my job. You say you want to be in a relationship with me, that you love me. Well, how on earth would that ever work if you'd flip out every time I leave the house?"

"Well, not every time."

She rolled her eyes. "You know what I mean."

Yeah, he did. And he had no clue what the answer was. "I don't know."

"Well, I can't wait around while you figure it out. I've got a job to do. But I'll tell you this—if you think you're going to stand in my way, you can say goodbye to this friendship, and to anything else that there might be between us."

His head snapped up. "Are you saying there is something more, that you do have feelings for me?"

She shrugged. "I guess it doesn't matter now. I put up with my father and the chauvinistic guys at the academy, but I'm not going to go into a relationship with someone that has that kind of attitude. I'm done."

Hope and fear tangled within him. If there was a chance, if she really was ready to take a leap of faith and see what happened, he'd be a fool to mess that up. But could he let himself be with her, love her and let her walk into harm's way on a regular basis?

"Like I said, I can't wait around while you figure it out." She opened the door, striding out into the twilight.

In two long strides he made it to the doorway, and called after her. "Sam!"

She paused, one foot on the running board of her truck, the door already open.

"Be safe. And call me later—I want to hear how it turns out."

She considered, probably wondering if he really wanted to know, or just wanted to check up on her. Honestly, it was a bit of both.

"It might be late."

"I don't care. I'll wait as long as it takes."

Sam carefully closed the door of her truck, making as little noise as possible. She'd parked a half mile away from the address the caller had given her; hopefully that was far enough. She needed every advantage going into a situation like this and wanted to scope out the scene without alerting anyone to her presence. The caller hadn't given much information, no indication of how many people were involved, or who they were. Just a message that the poachers had bagged another deer, and an address.

Most of the people in Paradise lived in the suburbs that covered the eastern portion of the island, but there were still some older, more rural places on the western part, bordering the wildlife preserve. That's where she was headed now. A drainage ditch ran along the side of the road, and although it would hold several feet of water in the summer, it was dry this time of year.

She slipped down the embankment and found that if she stuck to the middle, the brush offered decent cover. Making her way toward the house, she kept her eyes peeled for snakes and tried to figure out who could have called. It had been a woman, she was sure of that, but the voice wasn't familiar. It hadn't sounded like anyone she'd met on the island so far. Maybe an angry wife who'd decided to turn her spouse in? That was a reach, but with nothing to go on, it was as good a guess as any.

It took longer than she'd wanted to find the right address. Several times she'd scrambled up out of the ditch to check her bearings, keeping her head low as she scanned the surroundings. The fourth time, she found what she was looking for, a small, one-story house with wooden siding and a detached garage. Several vehicles were in the drive, including two pickup trucks. One of them tickled her memory, but the model was common enough it could belong to anyone.

The property backed right up to the reserve; that would be her best approach. Half climbing, half sliding into the gully again, she backtracked to a spot where she could cross into the woods out of eyeshot from the house.

Brambles and vines grabbed at her as she pushed her way through the underbrush that had grown up between the tall sand pines. Controlled burns couldn't be done this close to inhabited areas and invasive Brazilian pepper plants grew thickly here. Hard to hike through, but they offered excellent cover from which to observe the property. Crouching down behind the sheltering branches, she peered through high-powered binoculars, bringing the property into focus.

From this vantage point, she could see right into the open garage. There seemed to be only two men in the structure, one standing near the open doorway and another in front of a long, plastic-draped table. Hanging from a chain behind him was the partially-skinned car-cass of a deer. Switching from the binoculars to her camera, she shot off a series of photos, making sure to document the license plate on the truck closest to her. The other was facing the wrong way, but she noted down the make, model and color.

Her pulse sped—this was the most dangerous moment. She was going to have to make contact and hope no one decided it was open season on wildlife officers. Every recruit knew stories of those that had been killed in the line of duty and Sam had no desire to become the next cautionary tale. But she also wasn't going to let her natural nerves keep her from her duty to uphold the law.

Hand on her weapon, she eased out of the tree cover and announced herself. "Hey, what do you have there?"

The man closest to the door turned, and her stomach sank. It was Beau, the man she'd bested at the shooting range. She'd liked him, damn it. Now she was going to have to arrest him. So much for being a good judge of character.

"Hey, Beau, good to see you again." Better to keep things friendly if she could, but inside her temper was rising. He'd lied to her face, and she'd believed every word.

"Officer Finley." He nodded politely, his eyes darting to the man still standing inside the garage.

"And who's your friend here?"

"Oh, that's Donald, but he's not my friend, ma'am. I just met him today, over at the diner."

"Uh-huh. That true, Donald?"

The other man nodded, fear in his eyes. Fear wasn't good; people who were scared did dumb things. "Can you come over here, Donald, so we can chat without me having to shout? I don't want to annoy the neighbors, and it just doesn't feel friendly when I have to yell across the room, you know?"

"Um, okay." He stepped closer, and she got a better look at him. He was short and thin, not much older than herself. Late twenties, maybe? He had a thin, wispy excuse for a mustache under a pointed nose, and mousy brown hair that was already thinning at the temples. His tank top and dirty jeans were spattered with blood from the deer he'd begun butchering, as was the knife on the table.

"Thanks, Donald. I appreciate it." She smiled, wanting to put him at ease. An arrest was going to happen, but the easy way was a lot nicer than the hard way, for everyone involved. "You've got a nice setup here. I can tell you really know what you're doing."

Some of the tension went out of his shoulders—everyone liked to be told they were doing a good job, even when what they were doing was against the law. "Thanks, I found some videos online about how to rig up everything."

"Well, you did great. Unfortunately, given that deer season hasn't quite started yet, I'm going to have to charge you guys. You know that, right?"

Donald hung his head. "Yeah, I know. I just figured it was only a few weeks away, so it wasn't that big a deal. And my mom's been sick, and with me being out of work right now, the extra meat would come in handy."

"I hear you, but I'm afraid that doesn't excuse you from following the law. There are reasons we have limits on when and how you can hunt. As for the meat, that will be seized, and donated to a local charity."

"What? Oh, man. What about the antlers? I was going to hang that rack on my wall."

"Those are evidence, too, I'm sorry."

The man scuffed a worn shoe in the dirt, clearly more upset over the loss of his trophy than the loss of the meat. Probably because he had a freezer-full from the doe he'd killed the other day. She'd be checking that out and having his tires compared to the tracks left at the scene. But even if she couldn't tie him to the previous incident, she had him on hunting out of season, for sure.

"All right, I'm going to need a statement about where and when you two bagged the deer, and then I'm going to look around and secure the evidence."

Donald looked up, puzzled. "Us two? He—" he jabbed a thumb toward Beau, who'd been standing by silently in the doorway until now "—didn't shoot anything. I met him at the diner on my way home, and he asked if he could come by. Said he might be interested in buying some of the meat."

"That true, Beau?"

"Well…yes and no. I told him I wanted some meat, but that's just so's I could check things out. I remembered what you'd said about a poacher on the island, and when I saw he was telling the truth I sent a text to my wife, asking her to call you. I'd have called myself, but I didn't want him to hear me and pack everything up."

"Wait, the tip came from you? You're not one of the poachers?"

"Me? Heck, no. I hear they can take your guns away if you get caught poaching. It's not worth it. I can wait another few weeks. Hell, I still got meat in the freezer from last season."

Relief washed over her. She hadn't misjudged the big man. In fact, he might have saved her job. It would be a lot harder for her boss to find fault if she had a fresh arrest to put on his desk.

"You're gonna take my guns? That can't be legal!" Donald moved closer, his face red with anger.

Sam moved her hand to her gun, resting it on the butt of the weapon. "Donald, I need you to calm down, okay? So far, this is just a hunting violation, a misdemeanor. You add in assaulting an officer, and you're looking at a felony charge and real jail time. Who's going to take care of your mom then?"

He stopped, and she could almost see the wheels turning as he thought it through. Finally, he nodded. He'd been beat, and he knew it.

By the time her backup arrived, she'd gotten statements from both men, and after she'd found a stash of fresh venison in the freezer, Donald had broken down and admitted to the poaching incident with the doe. She'd also talked a little more to Donald about some of the services available to him, and Beau had offered some of the meat from his own freezer to the younger man and his mother. "Like I said, I still got plenty left over from last year. No reason not to share it if you need it."

Touched, she pulled him aside before he left. "I just wanted to thank you for calling in the tip, and for offering to help out Donald. You're a good guy."

He smiled, his grizzled features looking almost friendly. "That's how we do things around here. We help each other out. He's had some hard times, and he made some mistakes, but we all do, right? The problem is when you keep doing the same fool thing over and over again."

She mulled that over, her own choices flashing through her head. Was that her issue? Was she repeating the same "fool things," rather than learning from them? "You know, Beau, I think maybe you're right. So thanks, for everything."

"Like I said, around here, we help each other out. All you have to do is ask."

Driving home under the starlit sky, Sam felt like a million tons of weight had been lifted off her shoulders. Nabbing the poacher was a large part of it, but even better, the key to solving the case had come from someone in the community. And not one of Dylan's friends, but someone she'd impressed all on her own. Earning the respect of someone like Beau meant everything, both for her job and her own confidence.

For so long, she'd been told that being a woman would make this job hard, if not impossible. Not only did people assume she wouldn't be fit enough for the day-to-day difficulties, but also underneath that they implied that the hunting and fishing community wouldn't accept her authority. She'd tried to block out the naysayers, but deep down, she'd wondered and worried if they were right. What if she wasn't good enough? What if she couldn't stay strong in the heat of the moment? What if the people she encountered refused to accept her?

The old insecurities she'd harbored as a child had found new expressions in these adult worries, but tonight, finally, she could see them for what they were. Ghosts of her past, not predictions of the future. She'd stood on her own feet today, defused a dicey situation and generally kicked butt. Which, given how hard she'd worked for this moment, shouldn't be a shock, but it was. Despite what she'd been telling herself, the person who had doubted her abilities the most wasn't her father, or Dylan, but herself.

If she'd really thought she was good enough, she would never have suggested a fake relationship with Dylan. She had been so sure she wasn't enough on her own that she'd lied just to ride on his coattails. Then, when he'd asked for more, she'd shut him down, rather than believe she had what it took to make a relationship work. She'd underestimated Dylan, the people of Paradise and most of all herself.

But no more. As Beau had said, the shame wasn't in making mistakes, but in repeating them. The unlikely philosopher's words had resonated. She could change— she didn't have to do the same "fool" things over and over again. And she'd done a lot of foolish things lately. Starting with how she'd treated Dylan. She'd blown hot and cold with him so many times it was a miracle he still spoke to her at all. He deserved more than that. Hell, *she* deserved more than that. Maybe they wouldn't work out. Maybe he wouldn't be able to handle the risks of her job. Maybe she wasn't cut out for love. But damn it, she deserved the chance to find out.

Suddenly, tomorrow seemed too long to wait. Turning off the main road, she cut through a back street and headed back the way she'd come. Dylan lived only a few streets over from where she'd arrested Donald, and within minutes she was parked in front of his house, her heart racing at the thought of what she was about to do. Or try to do. Being open about her feelings wasn't going to be easy, but if anyone was worth it, he was.

The porch light was off, but a dim light flickered behind the blinds. Holding tight to her courage, she knocked firmly on the front door and waited. From somewhere in the woods, an owl called, looking for his mate. Maybe it was a night for love.

Shuffling footsteps, and then a muttered curse filtered through the solid wood of the cabin walls. Then the lock turned and Dylan was standing there, his eyes half-closed as he rubbed his elbow.

"Hi, did I wake you?" She should have called, but this was something she needed to do in person, before she chickened out.

"Sam? What are you doing here?"

"I wanted to see you, and I was in the area...but it's late. I can just talk to you another time—"

"No, wait, don't go." He scrubbed a hand across the stubble on his face. "I was just surprised, that's all. I was waiting up for you to call, but I guess I dozed off. Come in, please."

Butterflies dive-bombed in her stomach, but she nodded and followed him inside. "Is your elbow okay?"

He looked down to where he was still absently rubbing it. "What? Oh, yeah. I tripped over Toby and banged it on the wall."

The beagle wagged his tail, happy to hear his name, no matter the context.

"Oh, sorry."

"It's fine, really." He eased down onto the couch and muted the television with a flick of the remote. "So, what is it you wanted?"

She looked down at him, all hard lines and lean muscles, his hair mussed from sleep, his chin covered in stubble. He was the most gorgeous man she'd ever seen, had the mind of a genius and took in elderly dogs. He supported and understood her. He might even love her. And he had waited up just to hear that she was okay. He was everything she'd wanted, everything she'd been waiting for. "You. I wanted you."

His eyes dilated, the soft ocean blue turning stormy at her words. Heat pooled inside her; she wanted this man like she'd never wanted anything before. All her hard won self-control was gone, and in its place was a burning need to touch and be touched, to love him with her body the way she'd come to love him with her heart.

Kneeling beside him on the couch, she brushed his lips with hers, getting the faintest taste of him before moving to the line of his jaw. She kept trailing kisses toward his ear as he eased her into his lap. Straddling him, she could feel his excitement, and her own doubled in response. Panting, she sat upright and worked the buttons of her shirt, exposing more flesh with each flick of her fingers.

Moaning his appreciation, Dylan traced the edge of her bra with his finger, exploring her curves, then working his way down her rib cage. She arched toward him, practically purring, every nerve lighting up with pleasure.

Parting the rough fabric of her uniform, he pushed the material down her arms and leaned in to nibble at her collarbone. Lust jolted through her, and she had to grab ahold of his shoulders to keep from falling to the floor.

Dylan stilled, his oral exploration halted, as he ran a finger along a sore spot on her neck. "What's this?"

"Hmm?" She tipped her head back, giving him better access, trying to encourage him to go back to what he'd been doing.

"This." He probed again, and she winced. "Sam, you're bleeding. What the hell happened out there tonight?"

The harshness of his words cut through the hormones fogging her mind. Reaching up, she found a scrape about an inch long just below her ear. "It's nothing, a scratch. I'll be fine." She leaned in to him, shifting her hips to better position herself. "Better than fine if you kiss me again."

Instead, he lifted her off him and stood. "I'm serious, Sam. Why are you bleeding? You said you'd be safe, that you could take care of yourself, and you show up on my doorstep in the middle of the night looking like someone tried to take your head off. What the hell is going on?"

Passion flamed to anger in the space of a heartbeat. "What's going on is that I drove over here ready to tell you I love you, that I want to be with you, to make love to you. But because I scraped myself on a branch in the woods, I guess we're going to fight instead." She buttoned her shirt, her fingers fumbling as her heart raced.

Dylan startled, then reached for her. "Damn it, Sam, I don't want to fight."

"Neither do I." She finished the last button and squared her shoulders. "But if you can't handle my job, if you can't handle who I am, then this isn't going to work. I know that I made you wait while I figured things out, and I know you were patient with me. So I'll give you the same courtesy. Take some time, Dylan. Figure out if this is something you really want, because I'm not going to change. I'm going to work odd hours, and come home late, and I'm going to face situations that you don't like. You're going to have to trust that I can handle myself, or this won't work. I'm finally sure of myself, and I can't be with someone who isn't."

"Sam, wait."

She opened the door and looked at him, loving him even as she was leaving. "I will, but not forever."

Dylan pushed his way through the crowd blocking the stairs of the Sandpiper Inn. This was the first year that Jillian and Nic had hosted the Outdoor Days Festival and the turnout was amazing. In decades past, the grounds had been the default site for all the community gatherings, but for nearly a decade it had been allowed to fall into disrepair. The new owners were determined to restore it to its former glory, and from what he could see they had succeeded.

Games had been set up on the lawn, as well as booths selling fishing paraphernalia, baked goods and local artwork. Yesterday there had been a demonstration by a sharpshooter and today an archery club had offered free lessons. Down on the beach, some of the oldest residents had volunteered their time to help school children learn to fish, patiently demonstrating how to bait a hook and cast a line. Dylan had brought some of the more tame residents of the rehab center for the kids to see and learn about. But the highlight had been the fish fry put on by the fire department. They had skinned, filleted and cooked hundreds of pounds of fish, serving it up hot with piles of crisp coleslaw and tender hush puppies. He'd eaten way too much, but it was for charity, so justifiable in his book.

The only part of the weekend that hadn't gone well was his personal life. Somehow he'd ended up on both the setup and cleanup crews, on top of his own work with the booth the rehab center ran. The few times he'd managed to break away, Sam had been busy. He hadn't gotten to speak one word with her since she'd left his house Friday night, and if he didn't find her soon he was going to lose his mind.

Pushing down the steps got him a few dirty looks, but whatever. He had bigger things on his mind. He'd spotted Sam's khaki uniform over by the stage where a local bluegrass band was playing. A handful of people was dancing on the small dance floor, but most were spread out on blankets watching the band. He scanned the crowd, but Sam wasn't there. He'd missed her again. Turning back the way he came, he caught a glimpse of dark hair out of the corner of his eye.

There! She was standing with an older man dressed in khaki pants and a button-down shirt, easily the most formally dressed person at the festival. Her boss? Possibly, but he wasn't going to risk losing her again. He could be polite and professional, but he wanted her to know he was thinking about her. That he supported her. And if he smelled like cooking grease, that was just too bad.

"Sam, there you are! I've been looking all over for you."

She turned, and her smile assured him he'd made the right decision. He'd been dead on his feet, but one look at her had him ready for anything. "Hi, Dylan. This is my boss, Art Sanders. He's in charge of the entire region, and I was just thanking him for taking the time to come out here today."

Dylan shook hands with him, noting his no-nonsense expression. "Hello, Mr. Sanders. It's so nice that you could be here. Sam's really impressed us here in Paradise with all her hard work."

"You bet she has." Dani bumped him out of the way and offered a hand to the older man. "She's becoming such a vital part of the community, wouldn't you say, Dylan?"

"Absolutely. I don't know what I—I mean we, the community—would do without her."

Sam blushed. "Really guys, you don't have to say—"

"What she means is, I've already heard as much. Over

and over in fact. I've had more people talk to me about Sam than I can count." Art turned to her, a sparkle in his eye. "It seems you've really blossomed here in Paradise. In fact, I'd like to talk to you about an opportunity that's come across my desk. I was waiting to do it in private, but it seems privacy is hard to come by today."

Oops. "I'm sorry, I can come back later." Dylan backed up a step and trampled on Dani's foot.

"Um, me, too." She elbowed him and started to move off.

"No, no, I don't think it's anything Officer Finley would mind you hearing. I'm assuming you two are more of her friends? She seems to have made quite a few of them in her short time here. More than I'd expected, I have to say." He cleared his throat. "Anyway, I've received a request from the county to select someone to serve on an interdepartmental task force. It seems that there have been complaints about certain difficulties women face in the law enforcement community, and the idea is to create a mentor system. You'd be working with women from the sheriff's department, and there is talk of including the fire department, as well. Fields where men have tended to dominate."

"What about the legal field?" Dani piped up. "Women from the district attorney's office, public defenders, that kind of thing? They have to deal with mostly male judges, as well as male law enforcement officers. It can get pretty dicey sometimes."

"That's certainly something to consider. I can forward the idea to the county if you'd like, Ms....?

"Post. Dani Post. I'm a public defender with Palmetto County. I'd be very interested in helping, if Sam doesn't mind me tagging along."

"Mind? I think it's an incredible idea." She smiled up at her boss, confidence radiating off her. "I think the task force is exactly what we need, and I think the more women we can organize, the better. I'd be honored to take part."

She started tossing out ideas, and Dylan couldn't help but notice how much she'd changed. Gone was the person who'd hid her insecurities behind a false bravado, and in her place was a woman who knew her mind and her place in the world. She'd worried about everyone else's opinions, but it was her acceptance of herself that had made all the difference. She had done it on her own—she didn't need him. But that didn't mean he wasn't going to do his best to stand by her, if she'd have him.

"It was good seeing you, Officer Finley. Keep up the good work, and I'll let the County Commissioners know that you'll be representing our organization on the task force."

Sam thanked him again and breathed a sigh of relief. Her job was safe. Even better, she was going to have a chance to help change things for women like her. She had the support of the community and her boss. Now she just needed to know where Dylan stood.

Grabbing his arm, she started to pull him toward the steps to the beach. "Can I talk to you a second, alone?" She offered a smile of apology to Dani. "You don't mind, right?"

"Hey, never let it be said I stood in the path of true love. Y'all go make up or whatever you need to do."

Would they be making up? Or was her job just too much for him to deal with? She'd learned in the academy that a career in law enforcement made relationships difficult; maybe this just wasn't meant to be. But she *wanted* it to work, and she was pretty sure he did, too. That had to count for something, right?

"Hello, Sam."

It couldn't be. But it was. Her father. "Dad? What on earth are you doing here?" He never left the house for anything other than work, ever. She would have been less surprised if a mythical swamp ape had crawled out of the Everglades and come to visit.

He glanced around, visibly uncomfortable. "Maybe this was a mistake."

"Maybe. But you're here now, so out with it. What on earth got you to leave your little hole in the woods and come to Paradise?"

He looked at her with surprise and a new show of respect. She'd never spoken to him like that before, like an equal. Taking a deep breath, he pointed to her. "You did. I came for you, because I have some things to say to you that I should have talked about a long time ago."

Great. Now he wasn't satisfied with lecturing her in private, and he was going to do it in public. "Dad, I don't think this is the right time or place. How did you even know I would be here?"

"A friend of mine called, an old hunting buddy by the name of Beau Griggson. He told me about some run-ins you and he had, and that you were really making a name for yourself out here. Said I ought to come see for myself what a good job you were doing." His voice cracked. "He said you were doing me and your mama proud."

Were those tears in her father's eyes? She'd never seen him cry; she didn't know he could.

"And let me tell you something, Samantha. He was right. I've been watching you today, and I've talked to some people who I haven't seen in ten years or more. And every one of them told me how good you've been doing, and how glad they are that you're back here in Paradise."

She shaded her eyes and looked up at him. "What about you, Dad? Are you glad I moved back? Because I have to say it hasn't felt like it."

"Honey, I never wanted you to leave in the first place."

Her jaw dropped open. "How can you say that? You're the one that sent me away. My mom died, and you were so eager to be rid of me that you sent me to live with strangers." Now she was the one crying.

"Sam, I know you might not understand, but I hated it when you left. I wanted to keep you with me, but I was a mess. Your mom was my strength and my life, and when she died I didn't know how to go on. I was barely functioning, and there was no way I could take care of you the way your mom would have wanted. And I didn't want you to pay the price for my weakness. I thought boarding school would give you some normalcy and help you get over what had happened. Then, whenever you came to visit, I felt so guilty over failing you that I didn't know what to say or do. So I didn't say anything. You know how much I hate weakness, but I was weak and it drove us apart."

Sam stood, her head spinning from everything he'd said. Could it be true that he hadn't wanted her gone, that he'd missed her as much as she'd missed him? Shaking her head, she pushed back. "What about telling me I shouldn't join the FWC, that I wasn't good enough because I was a girl? You've never supported me in my career, ever."

"And I was wrong, obviously. You've done so well for yourself. But you have to understand, it's not that I didn't think you were good enough—it's that I didn't want you to be good enough. When you joined the academy, I was terrified. I know how dangerous this job can be, and I couldn't handle the thought of losing you. I thought if I could discourage you even a little, you'd find something else. Something safer."

"That's not fair, Dad. I can't live my life in a bubble just so you don't have to worry." Were all the men in her life destined to be overprotective? First Dylan, now her father. Although technically, her dad had been first, and she just hadn't known that was the motive behind his behavior. Still this argument was starting to feel like déjà vu. "Could I get hurt on the job? Sure. But I could also be hit by a bus on my way home tonight. I can't let the fear of what-if ruin my life. At the end of the day, you need to trust that I'm a grown woman, I'm well trained and I can handle myself."

"I get that now. I do. Seeing you today, in uniform, I'm not scared, I'm proud. And I know maybe it's too little, too late, but I'd like to start over. Maybe have you over for dinner next week, so we can get to know each other again?"

"I'd like that. But let's get pizza like we used to." Maybe they couldn't recapture the closeness of her youth, but it was a good start.

"Officer Finley, they need you up onstage. It's the closing ceremonies." Wow, was it that time already? She glanced at her watch, then looked for Dylan, but he'd disappeared, probably to give her some privacy while she talked to her father. She'd have to hunt him down during the cleanup tonight.

"Dad, I've got to go, but thanks. I'm glad you came." Impulsively, she gave him a quick hug, then dashed toward the stage before her traitorous emotions could overwhelm her again.

* * *

Dylan watched the stage from the steps below as the mayor thanked all the people who had helped make the festival happen. Special thanks was given to the Fish and Wildlife Commission, the Paradise City Council, and the owners of the Sandpiper. Then a list of volunteers was read, and given how many people had worked on the project, most of the audience had been named by the time he was done.

Next were the awards. The mayor handed out trophies and ribbons for the most fish caught, the biggest catch, the winner of the archery competition, and the Overall Sportsman award for the child with the best combined scores from fishing and archery. The winner this year was a ten-year-old girl not much bigger than the enormous trophy she was presented with.

Now it was Dylan's turn at the microphone. He took the stairs two at a time, adrenaline and anticipation fueling his movement. Over the noise of the crowd, he could hear the mayor introducing him and the purpose of the Paradise Wildlife Rehabilitation Center. When the applause died down Dylan took the microphone and waved to the people below. "Hello, everyone! I want to thank everyone who purchased an item or a raffle ticket at our booth today, or made a donation. The animals we serve rely on your generosity—we couldn't do what we do without your help."

He waved to Sam, motioning her to join him. "I'm going to ask one of our own, local Fish and Wildlife Officer Sam Finley, to help me give away our raffle prizes." The crowd cheered, and Sam had no choice but to join him at the podium.

"Officer Finley, I have the winner tickets here. If you

could just read off the names in order, I'll handle the prizes."

Sam took the brightly colored tickets and read the first name into the microphone. A cheer went up from the back of the crowd, and Grace Keville, the owner of Sandcastle Cakes Bakery, made her way to the stage.

"Here you go, courtesy of local photographer Mollie Post." He handed her a framed print of the beach at sunrise, and she took her seat, beaming.

"The next winner is…Missy Cunningham!" Another winner came forward, claiming a certificate for a weekend stay at the Sandpiper Inn. Sam continued to call names as Dylan handed out prizes, everything from a custom-made fishing rod to a sunset dinner cruise. Finally, there was just one ticket left.

Sam stared at the name on the slip, then looked at Dylan in confusion. "This has my name on it."

He nodded, unable to hold back a smile. "I know."

She shook her head. "But I didn't enter any of the raffles."

He stepped closer, his hand gripping the ring in his pocket. "I know. And I'm not much of a prize, but this was the best idea I could come up with on short notice."

The crowd went silent, sensing that this wasn't part of the scheduled program.

"Sam Finley, you have had me head over heels since you held me at gunpoint in the woods." Laughter floated up from the crowd as Sam's eyes widened. "I am so proud of you and what you have accomplished, not just this weekend with the festival, but every day. You risk your life to protect this special place, and I can't imagine a better person for the job. I know I haven't been as supportive as I could be, but I promise you, that's going to change. I'm going to stand behind you. The truth is, Paradise needs you, doesn't it?"

A cheer went up from the crowd, with a few catcalls and fox whistles thrown in. Sam blushed, but he could tell she still didn't know where this was going. It was time to clear things up. Sinking to one knee, he pulled the ring from his pocket, letting the sun's rays catch the deep blue of the single sapphire.

"What's more, I need you. I want to have you in my life, every day, for the rest of my life."

Sam covered the microphone with her hand, panic in her eyes. "Are you crazy? You don't have to do this. My job's safe. I'm not going anywhere."

He grinned, hoping the love and pride he felt would shine through somehow. "I know I don't have to. I want to. This isn't about your job or a fake relationship. It's about how I feel when I'm with you. Well, that, and about how awful I feel when we're apart."

Turning to the crowd, he yelled, "I think I need a little help here!"

A heckler in the back, probably Dani, yelled, "Sam, make him beg!" but then, one by one, the people in the front row held up cards, each with a single word on it, spelling out WILL YOU MARRY ME?

Sam's mouth dropped open, and Dylan thought his heart was going to pound right out of his chest. This was it, the moment he'd been waiting for.

"So, Sam, what do you say? Are you ready to take a chance on me?"

Sam couldn't believe her eyes. Dylan had a ring? An engagement ring? And he'd gotten other people in on his scheme? Closing her eyes, she willed herself to wake up, but when she opened them again he was still there, love and hope shining in his eyes.

From below, chants of "say yes" started to grow, and she found herself inexplicably laughing. As a girl, she'd imagined a proposal to be something very serious and private, but somehow this felt right. She'd fallen in love not just with Dylan, but with the people of Paradise, and it was only fitting that they were all in this together. Crazy, but fitting.

Actually, the idea of getting married at all was crazy. They'd only known each other such a short time. But waiting around hadn't gotten her anywhere in life, and deep down she knew her feelings were real. "I love you, too, Dylan. I have ever since I saw you holding that orphan deer, and I always will. So yes, I'll marry you."

She felt him slip the cool band over her finger, and then he was back on his feet, lifting her into his arms. This time, there was nothing to keep them apart, no fear to spoil things. Just love, and a sense of finally being exactly where she belonged.

Below them the crowd roared in approval, and somehow the band started playing again, this time a bluegrass version of a wedding march, as Dylan escorted her off the stage.

She'd barely stepped foot on the ground when she was sideswiped by a huge hug. "I can't believe it! You're engaged!" Dani squeezed hard, then let her go to inspect the ring. "This is gorgeous. Dylan, you did good."

"Thanks," he drawled, putting a protective arm around Sam. "The sapphire reminds me of the ocean and Paradise, but if you want a diamond, we can shop for something more traditional."

"Are you kidding? I love it." She watched the play

of light within the facets, so similar to the reflection of the waves in the waters that surrounded the island. "It's perfect. But when on earth did you get this?" She'd only realized her feelings for him a few days ago, and they'd both been busy with the festival ever since.

A sheepish grin tipped his features. "It's actually a family heirloom. I had my mom bring it with her so I could give it to you. But I can buy you something else. You don't have to keep it."

She narrowed her eyes. "Just try to get it off of me."

She felt someone pull at her shirt, and looked down to find at her feet a munchkin of a little girl with strawberry blonde pigtails. Behind her was Cassie, a tiny baby asleep in her arms.

"Well, you must be Emma. You look just like your mother."

"Uh-huh. And I have to tell you something."

"Okay, honey, what is it?"

"I'm six years old, and I'm going to be your flower girl."

Sam tried to hold back her laughter, but a small chuckle burst through. She'd been engaged for less than five minutes and already had her first attendant. Weren't brides supposed to be the pushy ones?

Cassie grabbed Emma with her free hand, pulling her away. "Emma!"

Emma looked up at her mom, her blue eyes wide with innocence. "What? I'm always the flower girl. I just wanted to make sure Officer Sam knew."

Cassie winced, but Jillian, standing right beside her laughed out loud. "She has a point, Cass."

"Well, then, we wouldn't want to break with tradition." Sam winked at the little girl. "It might be bad luck."

"Hurray!" Satisfied, Emma skipped off toward her father, who'd been standing at the edge of the group.

"Sorry about that." Cassie gave her an apologetic smile.

"Not at all. I'm flattered she wants to be a part of it."

"We all want to be a part of it," Jillian said. "You have to at least let us help you plan. We can have another girls' night, and look at bridal magazines, and pick out your colors, and—"

"Whoa, give the girl a break!" Mollie pushed her way into the crowd of women. "She's going to change her mind and elope if you guys don't back off a bit."

"My baby girl isn't going to elope, not if I have anything to say about it." Her dad's grin, rusty from disuse, warmed her heart. "I want to walk you down the aisle, if you'll let me."

She nodded, blinking back happy tears.

"What's this about eloping?" From around the side of the stage came Dylan's family, some of them still holding signs from his crazy proposal. His mother gave her a kiss on the cheek, taking her place in the gathering. "I was hoping you might want to get married on the ranch."

"Actually, I think I'd like to do it here, on the island. A way to bring things full circle and really mark that I'm home for good." She looked up at Dylan. "Unless Dylan really wants to do it on the ranch."

"What I want is a few minutes with my fiancée. Alone. We'll catch up with the rest of you later."

Without another word, he steered her down a sandy path between the trees. She turned to him. "Thank you. I love that everyone is so excited, but…"

"But they can be overwhelming. Yeah. Welcome to

Paradise. You'll get used to it." He urged her to walk faster, and as they came out of the trees she gasped.

"How beautiful…it's like something out of a fairy tale." In front of her, the trail led through an open field full of wildflowers to a white gazebo with a high-peaked roof. Behind that was an unobstructed view of the ocean. Stepping into the late afternoon sunshine with Dylan by her side was like stepping into a storybook. Except this was her life now, her very own happily-ever-after.

She entered the gazebo, marveling at the ornateness of the woodwork. "This is gorgeous."

Dylan nipped at her neck, sending delicious shivers down her spine. "Not half as gorgeous as you. I can't believe you're going to be mine."

She twisted in his arms, rising up on tiptoe to find his lips. One long, sultry, soul-stirring kiss later, she leaned dreamily against him. "I don't ever want to move. Let's stay here forever."

"I like the forever part, but at some point I think we might get hungry."

"Mmm, good point."

He traced the shell of her ear with his finger, tickling and seducing at the same time. "Speaking of forever, do you have anything you really want, as far as the wedding goes? I'm afraid if we don't make up our minds quickly, our friends and family will plan it all without us."

She opened her eyes and took in the tropical beauty around her. "How about here?"

"On the island, you mean?"

"I mean here, in this gazebo. It's perfect. Wild, yet beautiful."

"Just like you." He kissed her again, and her toes curled.

"And I think we should do it soon. I know it sounds crazy, but I feel like I've been waiting my whole life for you, and I don't want to wait anymore." She ran a fingernail across the skin at the open neck of his shirt. "Think you can handle a short engagement?"

He growled deep in his throat, the vibrations sending new waves of need through her. "Baby, I'd marry you this minute if I could. Just tell me when, and I'll be there."

Chapter Sixteen

A month to plan a wedding turned out to be the bare minimum, but even that felt too long. Between her work and Dylan's, the new women's task force, and the actual wedding preparation, she felt like they'd barely had any time alone since the day he'd proposed.

But the little time they had they had made the most of, with stolen kisses in the corner of the grocery store and long nights curled up on the couch while she considered menus and seating charts and he wrangled spreadsheets. She'd asked him time and again what he would like to incorporate into their wedding, but every time he simply said "you."

Which meant she'd had free rein to make today the wedding of her dreams. Thankfully, the Sandpiper had been available, and Jillian had gone to great lengths to make sure everything was ready on such short notice.

It helped that they had decided on a small, simple ceremony. One attendant each, immediate family and their closest friends. All the people that mattered to them, with the exception of one. Her mom.

As if reading her mind, her father took her hand. "You look every bit as beautiful as your mother did in that dress. I know she'd be so happy that you chose to wear it."

Sam looked down at the simple white dress, one of the few things her father had held on to after her mother died. Short on time, she'd been panicking about getting a dress until her father had shown up at her apartment with it one evening, unannounced. She'd instantly fallen in love with it and miraculously it had only needed a few alterations to fit like it had been made of her. Sleeveless with a sweetheart neckline and an A-line skirt, it transformed her from tomboy to princess. Now she just needed to marry her prince. "Is everything set up?"

Dani, her maid of honor, gave a thumbs-up. "Just waiting on you, babe." Wearing a blue sheath dress the color of Sam's ring, Dani stood watch at the French doors leading from Jillian and Nic's bedroom out to the lawn.

"I guess this is it, then. Jessica, can you tell them I'm ready?"

"You got it." Since Jillian, Cassie and Mollie all had children to wrangle, Cassie's sister-in-law had been pressed into service, serving as a sort of lady-in-waiting. The younger woman had kept up such a stream of chatter, sometimes switching between English and Spanish, that Sam hadn't had a chance to feel nervous. And now it was too late for cold feet, not that she had them.

A moment passed, and then the sound of music filled the air.

"That's our cue, baby." Her father held out his arm,

and she took it, letting him lead her through the doors onto the sun-drenched patio. From there it was a short walk to the clearing, now transformed with folding white chairs set up in precise rows on either side of the path. And there, waiting for her on the steps of the gazebo, was Dylan.

Her lungs seized at the sight of him in his tuxedo, looking like he'd walked out of one of the pages of the wedding magazines she'd scoured. How was she supposed to keep her hands off him during the ceremony when he looked like that? Catching her eye, he winked, and she would have fallen if her father hadn't been there to steady her.

Somehow she made it down the aisle to Dylan, muffling a laugh when she realized Toby was waiting for her as well, apparently refusing to be left out of the fun. It was smooth sailing from there, and before she could catch her breath it was time to recite the vows they had written.

Dylan took both her hands in his, so impossibly handsome she was afraid she'd forget to breathe.

"Samantha Finley, I vow to love you, to listen to you, to stand by you come what may. I promise to be your friend, your partner and your lover, today and always. And most of all, I promise to try every day to be the kind of man that deserves a woman like you."

Tears filled her eyes, and a glance at their audience showed her she wasn't alone. Swallowing past the lump in her throat, she spoke.

"Dylan Turner, today I promise to spend my life with you, at your side, equal partners in life and love. I promise to share my hopes and dreams and fears with you, and never leave you in the dark. And most of all, I promise to love you with all my heart, because I know that it will always be safe with you."

Cheers rang out from the crowd, almost drowning out the minister's final words, but at last she heard the words she'd been waiting for.

"You may now kiss your bride."

And he did. So well and so thoroughly that she would have sworn her lips were still tingling hours later when Dylan carried her over the threshold of the cabin they'd rented for their honeymoon. Tonight she'd danced until her feet were sore, stuffed herself on barbecued brisket and cake and laughed until her sides hurt. But when she looked in her husband's eyes, she knew the best was yet to come.

* * * * *

Look out for the next
PROPOSALS IN PARADISE *story*
from Katie Meyer,
coming in March 2017!

And don't miss Katie's previous
PARADISE ANIMAL CLINIC *romances,*
available only from Mills & Boon Cherish:
DO YOU TAKE THIS DADDY?
A VALENTINE FOR THE VETERINARIAN
THE PUPPY PROPOSAL

MILLS & BOON®

Cherish™

EXPERIENCE THE ULTIMATE RUSH OF FALLING IN LOVE

A sneak peek at next month's titles...

In stores from 20th October 2016:

- **Christmas Baby for the Princess** – Barbara Wallace *and* **The Maverick's Holiday Surprise** – Karen Rose Smith
- **Greek Tycoon's Mistletoe Proposal** – Kandy Shepherd *and* **A Child Under His Tree** – Allison Leigh

In stores from 3rd November 2016:

- **The Billionaire's Prize** – Rebecca Winters *and* **The Rancher's Expectant Christmas** – Karen Templeton
- **The Earl's Snow-Kissed Proposal** – Nina Milne *and* **Callie's Christmas Wish** – Merline Lovelace

MILLS & BOON®

EXCLUSIVE EXCERPT

When Dea Caracciolo agrees to attend a sporting event as tycoon Guido Rossano's date, sparks fly!

Read on for a sneak preview of
THE BILLIONAIRE'S PRIZE
the final instalment of Rebecca Winters'
thrilling Cherish trilogy
THE MONTINARI MARRIAGES

The dark blue short-sleeved dress with small red poppies Dea was wearing hugged her figure, then flared from the waist to the knee. With every step the material danced around her beautiful legs, imitating the flounce of her hair she wore down the way he liked it. Talk about his heart failing him!

"Dea—"

Her searching gaze fused with his. "I hope it's all right." The slight tremor in her voice betrayed her fear that she wasn't welcome. If she only knew...

"You've had an open invitation since we met." Nodding his thanks to Mario, he put his arm around her shoulders and drew her inside the suite.

He slid his hands in her hair. "You're the most beautiful sight this man has ever seen." With uncontrolled hunger he lowered his mouth to hers and began to devour her. Over the announcer's voice and the roar of the crowd, he heard her little moans of pleasure as their bodies merged and they drank deeply.

When she swayed in his arms, he half carried her over to the couch where they could give in to their frenzied needs. She smelled heavenly. One kiss grew into another until she became his entire world. He'd never known a feeling like this and lost track of time and place.

"Do you know what you do to me?" he whispered against her lips with feverish intensity.

"I came for the same reason."

Her admission pulled him all the way under. Once in a while the roar of the crowd filled the room, but that didn't stop him from twining his legs with hers. He desired a closeness they couldn't achieve as long as their clothes separated them.

"I want you, *bellissima*. I want you all night long. Do you understand what I'm saying?"

Don't miss
THE BILLIONAIRE'S PRIZE
by Rebecca Winters

Available November 2016

www.millsandboon.co.uk

Give a 12 month subscription to a friend today!

Call Customer Services
0844 844 1358*

or visit
millsandboon.co.uk/subscription